WASHOE COUNTY LIBRARY

3 1235 03668 7940

Lilly
and the
Pirates

D1005128

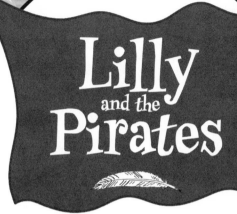

Lilly
and the
Pirates

Phyllis Root

Illustrations by Rob Shepperson

BOYDS MILLS PRESS
AN IMPRINT OF HIGHLIGHTS
Honesdale, Pennsylvania

For Jane, fellow pirate heart and true friend
  —PR

For Chris
  —RS

Text copyright © 2010 by Phyllis Root
Illustrations copyright © 2010 by Rob Shepperson
All rights reserved

For information about permission to reproduce selections from this book,
please contact permissions@highlights.com

Printed in the United States of America
Designed by Barbara Grzeslo
First paperback edition, 2013

Library of Congress Cataloging-in-Publication Data

Root, Phyllis.
Lilly and the pirates / Phyllis Root ; pictures by Rob Shepperson. — 1st ed.
p. cm.
Summary: Ten-year-old Lilly, a worrier who greatly fears the sea,
leaves the home of her librarian-great-uncle with an old woman pirate
to rescue her parents, who were shipwrecked while seeking
the elusive frangipani fruit fly on an uncharted island.
ISBN 978-1-59078-583-6 (hc) · ISBN 978-1-62091-027-6 (pb)
[1. Adventure and adventurers—Fiction. 2. Pirates—Fiction.
3. Worry—Fiction. 4. Self-realization—Fiction. 5. Sailing—Fiction.
6. Missing persons—Fiction.] I. Shepperson, Rob, ill. II. Title.
PZ7.R6784Lhm 2010
[Fic]—dc22
2009030494

Boyds Mills Press, Inc.
815 Church Street
Honesdale, Pennsylvania 18431

10 9 8 7 6 5 4 3 2 1

Lilly
and the
Pirates

RECEIVED

SEP 0 0 2013

NORTHWEST RENO LIBRARY
Reno, Nevada

Contents

The boat deck tilted under Lilly's feet. She teetered. The black water yawned beneath her.

Destinations

The hot wind sneaked in through the flap of the ragged canvas tent and rattled the pages of Lilly's book. She curled on her cot in a corner pretending to read *Millicent Murray and the Fish That Didn't Splash*. A new crate of books had just arrived by camelback and sat in the center of the tent floor. Usually Lilly couldn't wait to dive into the latest Millicent Murray mystery. What Lilly was really doing, though, was eavesdropping on her momma and poppa as they sat nearby reading and rereading the pages of the letter. The envelope had lain on top of the books when they pried off the lid of the wooden crate. Lilly had recognized the return address printed on the envelope: Scientific Institute, the college that sent them off on all their expeditions to the corners of the world.

Except, of course, the world didn't have corners. Lilly knew that. She knew the world was round, pear-shaped really, with a circumference of 24,901.55 miles at the equator. Just because Lilly had never gone to a real school didn't mean she didn't know things. Lots of things. The crates that followed them on their expeditions to the jungle or the desert or the tops of old volcanoes always contained schoolbooks along with scientific journals for her parents and any new Millicent Murray mysteries for Lilly. Lilly's poppa always said she was smarter than any two ten-year-olds he knew. He had said something like that ever since Lilly could remember. Smarter than any two four-year-olds. Smarter than any two five-year-olds. Lilly was seven before she realized Poppa didn't know any other seven-year-olds. How could he? It had always been just the three of them, Lilly and her momma and poppa, traveling together to study boomerang beetles or lily pad leeches or snowshoe mosquitoes.

Lilly's poppa lowered his voice, and Lilly leaned closer to hear. This was new, this whispering. Usually they told her straight out where they were going next.

"Do you think the frangipangi fruit fly has really been sighted?" he whispered. "There have been mistaken reports before."

"But if the reports are accurate—" Lilly's momma whispered back.

"And we have an opportunity to study them in their native habitat—"

"If only someone knew where that habitat was—"

"Maybe we could answer that question—"

"We've always dreamed that someday we would study them."

A soppy, sentimental look passed between her parents. Lilly knew about their dream. She had often heard how her parents had met—two extremely shy students whose hands accidentally touched at the library of the Scientific Institute as they both reached for the same book, *Frangipangi Fruit Fly: Fact or Fiction?* But why were they whispering? Something must be really dangerous about where they would be going next. Lilly reached for her worry book, always at her side, ready for her to scribble down any worries she might think of. If Lilly worried enough about all the things that could go wrong, if she wrote her worries down in her worry book, the bad things she worried about might not happen.

What Lilly wrote in her worry book was one of two secrets she kept from her momma and poppa. They were far too scientific to believe that worrying could keep disasters at bay. She had started her first worry book not long after the wave that had almost swept her momma and poppa away forever. She had found a blank notebook in a crate of books and drawn a picture of an enormous green wave curving menacingly over her momma and poppa. Then she had scribbled over the whole wave in black crayon, closed the book, and piled rocks on top of it. The next day she had cautiously pushed the rocks away and peeked inside. The wave was still there, still scribbled out. It hadn't escaped and tried to carry her momma and poppa away again.

That had been her first worry book, many worry books ago. Lilly couldn't explain why, but somehow writing down all the things that could go wrong inside the pages of a book, a book she could close, seemed to keep those dangers inside where they couldn't harm anyone, least of all her momma and poppa, who never seemed to understand all the disasters that might be lurking in wait for them.

But Lilly knew. Whatever genes had made her parents brave and fearless had skipped over Lilly. Pictures of all the things that could go terribly, dreadfully wrong loomed up in Lilly's mind like a giant curling wave.

An expedition to the Dire Desert? What if the camels got lost and sore-footed far from an oasis?

Research in the Mountains of No Return? What if a passing yodeler started an avalanche and buried them all?

Better to worry early and often to cover every disaster than to be sorry afterward. That was Lilly's motto.

Please, please, Lilly silently implored, *don't send us over the ocean.* Who knew what might be hiding under that dark, undulating surface? Giant squid? Bottomless whirlpools? Leeches the size of whales?

"If we do decide to accept—" Lilly's momma went on.

"—what would we do about Lilly?" finished Lilly's poppa.

Do about her? Lilly sat up straight on her cot. Why, take her along, of course. How else could she worry for them and keep them safe? She had always gone with them. Lilly and her momma and poppa. They were a family.

"Maybe it would be better—" whispered Lilly's momma.

"—if Lilly didn't go this time?" finished her poppa.

Left Behind

Lilly quit pretending not to eavesdrop.

"Not go?" she cried. "I have to go. I always go."

"Lilly, dear," began her poppa.

"You'd be miserable," said her momma.

"No, I won't," said Lilly. "I'll be with you."

"It's a long trip," said Lilly's momma.

"I've been on long trips before," Lilly argued. "All our trips are long trips."

"But this one is by boat," said her poppa. "I'm sorry, Lilly, but we think it's best if you don't go."

Lilly's momma reached out and wrapped an arm around Lilly. "Sweetie, we'd love for you to come with us. But remember how scared you got kayaking up the Torpid River?"

Lilly nodded.

"And how terrified you were when we had to wade across a stream on Mount Rushless?" said her poppa.

Lilly nodded again. She had made them all wear life jackets, even though the water came up only to their ankles. She herself had worn two life jackets.

Lilly took a deep breath. "I can do it now," she said. "I know I can." Somehow she would stand being on a boat, on water, for an hour or so if it meant not being left behind.

"Lilly," said her poppa, "this isn't just a short trip. It's days and days by boat."

"Over the ocean," added her momma.

Lilly's breath stuck in her throat. "I can do it," she said again, but even Lilly heard how her voice quavered.

"It's not just the boat trip," said her poppa. "We'll be spending all our time on islands. Small islands."

Islands had ocean all around them, with tides that went in and out so you were never sure if the water was creeping up on you or drawing you out onto the sand so it could wash over you again. Ocean with untrustworthy waves that curled up green and grinning and tried to steal away what you loved best in the world.

"Breathe, sweetie," said her poppa, rubbing the middle of Lilly's back.

"Lilly dearest, we love you too much to put you through all that," said her momma.

Lilly clutched her book. What would Millicent Murray do? She would go with them, of course. She would sail the ship herself. She would fight off dangers along the way and bring them safely to the islands. At the very least she would try to stow away on the boat if she was left behind.

Maybe Millicent Murray could do all that, but Lilly couldn't. She would die of fear, if such a thing were possible.

"Will I just wait here for you, then?" asked Lilly. She would be lonely, but she had a box full of new books. She had her worry books to fill. Where else could she go? They didn't have a house somewhere like the people in the books Lilly read. They had lived in tents and huts and hammocks all Lilly's life.

"Oh, sweetie," said her momma, "you're a big girl, but you're not that big."

"We couldn't leave you alone," said her poppa. "We're not sure how long we'll be gone, and we want to know you'll be safe."

What about you? Lilly wanted to ask. They wouldn't

be safe. They wouldn't even know how unsafe they were.

"Perhaps you could go to stay with your great-uncle Ernest in Mundelaine," said Lilly's momma. "He's all the family we have."

Great-Uncle Ernest? Lilly had never even met him.

"He was very kind to me as a child," said Lilly's momma. "We haven't seen him in years because Uncle Ernest never really goes anywhere at all. But I know he'll be glad to have you visit. I'll write to him and see if you can stay with him."

Lilly flung herself on her parents. "Don't go," she begged. "Do you have to go?"

"Well . . . ," said her poppa.

"I suppose if we had to turn it down . . . ," said her momma.

Lilly could read the look that passed between them and the slump of their shoulders as clearly as if they had been pages in a book.

She sighed. "I'll go to Great-Uncle Ernest's," she said.

"That's our Lilly!" Her poppa swept her up in a hug.

"Thank you, sweetie," said her momma, kissing the top of Lilly's head, which was all that stuck out of the hug. "It will be good practice for you. Before long, we'll be sending you off to the Scientific Institute to study."

Lilly couldn't help picturing herself being nailed up

in a crate and shipped off to the school. Should she tell them now? "There's something . . . ," she began. But her parents were already off in a flurry of plans.

"We'll need a boat," said her poppa.

"And copies of the reports of the sightings," said her momma.

"And homing sea gulls."

"And waterproof notebooks."

Lilly reached for her worry book. Her momma would write to Great-Uncle Ernest. Her poppa would write back to the institute and tell them they accepted the assignment. And Lilly would write all her worries down to try to keep her parents safe. She turned to a fresh page and then looked up. "Where exactly are you going?" she asked.

"Didn't we say?" asked her momma. "The Shipwreck Islands."

Lilly leaned over her worry book and wrote the worst worry she could think of.

What if Momma and Poppa didn't come back?

The Road to Mundelaine

L illy dragged her feet through the bus station. Now that the moment had come to say good-bye to her momma and poppa, she hoped fiercely that something would happen. Some miracle that would change her momma's and poppa's minds. It had been all rush and flurry for the past few days as they finished up the last of the experiments and packed up the tent, the equipment, and the books.

Lilly had dawdled as much as she dared, taking her time folding and refolding her clothes to put in her duffle bag. The tent had been the last thing to come down.

Lilly had carefully smoothed the tattered canvas. Here was the corner of the tent she had chewed when she was teething. There was the bend in the tent pole where she had tumbled when she was learning to walk.

But at last everything was ready. Camels carried them to a road, where a truck drove them to the nearest town, where awaiting them was a letter from Great-Uncle Ernest, written in neat, tiny handwriting: *I would be glad to have Lilly as a guest.* Then a new flurry of things to do: a boat to charter, bus schedules to check. While her parents made those arrangements, Lilly had stayed in the hotel room, filling page after page in her worry book. Bad enough that the town was a harbor town, with glimpses of the ocean from almost every street. By carefully avoiding the sight of the rolling waves, Lilly could keep breathing normally. And even though Great-Uncle Ernest lived in a city by the sea, too, her momma had assured her that his house was on an inland street, away from the water.

Now the time had finally come to say good-bye, and Lilly could hardly bear it. How could she get on the bus and leave them for the first time in her life? What if she changed her mind, begged them to stay?

But this was their dream. How could she ruin it for them? She would get on the bus and ride away, even though it was the hardest thing she had ever done. Her poppa sniffled, and her momma's eyes were wet.

Lilly's poppa hefted Lilly's bag up the steps into the bus.

"You'll be in Mundelaine before you know it," he said.

"And we'll be back before you even miss us," said Lilly's momma.

Lilly was sure that wasn't true, because she missed them already, and she hadn't even left yet. But she nodded to make them feel better.

"Now give us a hug and promise to be good as gold at Uncle Ernest's," said Lilly's poppa.

"I promise," she mumbled from the middle of the hug.

The bus driver honked his horn. Lilly clutched her parents one last time, climbed on the bus, found a seat, and yanked the bus window open. Gas fumes floated in. The bus started to roll.

"Good-bye, good-bye, we love you." Her momma and poppa waved wildly.

Lilly leaned out the window to be closer to them for just a minute longer. She thought of a new worry. "How will I know what Great-Uncle Ernest looks like?" Lilly called.

"He'll meet you at the station," Lilly's momma called back. "He's—"

The bus engine roared, and the bus pulled out of the station and rounded a corner. Lilly hunched back on the hard bus seat. Her momma and poppa were gone.

Streets, shops, and houses blurred by. The bus turned another corner and jounced onto the coast road to Mundelaine. Lilly looked out the far window, away from the treacherous ocean.

Soon Lilly's momma and poppa would be sailing on that sea, sailing over water so deep you couldn't see the bottom of it. Sailing away from Lilly. Lilly dug her worry book out of her bag. Worrying might take her mind off her troubles. *What if*, she wrote carefully.

The bus swerved, and Lilly's handwriting ran crooked, but she kept on writing. Away from her momma and poppa she could give her worries free rein. In the tent, it was easier to let them think she was writing down scientific observations in her notebook. Once in a while, Lilly even left it open to a page where she had made a drawing and entered some random notes, just to throw them off.

"You'll make a fine scientist someday," her poppa often told her.

"Who knows what you'll study at the institute?"

said her momma. "What kind of scientist you'll be?"

That was Lilly's second secret. Deep down inside, Lilly wasn't sure yet what she wanted to be, but in the back of her worry book, she kept a list of things she knew she didn't want to be. So far it was a short list: scientist. Maybe she would solve mysteries like Millicent Murray, although she knew she could never be that brave. Until she was sure, she didn't want to see the look of disappointment on her parents' faces when she told them she didn't want to go to the institute.

Lilly wrote down worry after worry. There was no end of them.

Pirates?

The bus lurched around a corner and into a bus station. Lilly peered out the bug-spattered window. What if Great-Uncle Ernest had gotten the day wrong and didn't meet her bus? What if she had somehow gotten on the wrong bus and ended up in the wrong city? What if the driver was a kidnapper in disguise? Lilly turned to a new page in her worry book.

"Mundelaine," the driver yelled.

Lilly gathered up her bag of blank notebooks and her favorite Millicent Murray mystery, *Millicent Murray and the Hyena That Didn't Laugh*. Lilly had wanted to bring all thirty-seven volumes (so far) of Millicent

Murray mysteries, but her momma had pointed out that Uncle Ernest was a librarian, in fact the chief librarian of Mundelaine. Surely Lilly would be able to check out books to her heart's content. Lilly loved how Millicent Murray did everything boldly, valiantly, intrepidly, stalwartly, fearlessly. A lot like Lilly's momma and poppa. Nothing frightened Millicent. If only Lilly could be a little more like Millicent Murray, maybe she could have gone along to the Shipwreck Islands. Of course, when Millicent's adventures became too scary, Lilly could always shut the book. And since next month a new Millicent Murray mystery would come out, it was a sure bet that no matter what dire adventures awaited Millicent, she would survive.

Lilly stepped down onto the oil-stained concrete and peered into the dank dimness of the bus station.

Only one person was waiting for the bus.

He wore a wide black hat with the brim pulled low, a patch on one eye, boots with silver buckles, and a brace of pistols stuck in the scarlet sash tied around his middle. In his hand he held an empty birdcage. But it was his ears Lilly noticed most of all. They stuck out from his head like tiny sails. A gold hoop pierced one of the ears. The man scowled at Lilly.

Her heart quavered. She had never, never in her life

thought to write in her worry book, *What if Great-Uncle Ernest is a pirate?*

"Uncle Ernest?" Lilly whispered.

"Lilly?"

The voice came from behind her. Lilly turned. Someone else was waiting for the bus. She hadn't even noticed him; he blended so into the gloom of the bus station in his gray suit and gray tie. A gray hat sat on his gray hair. Under his arm he held a thick gray book. Even his voice sounded gray, like dust motes floating up from the pages of an old book that hadn't been opened in years.

"You are Lilly, aren't you?" the man asked. "If so, I am your great-uncle Ernest."

Great-Uncle Ernest had opened his thick book to a page from which a bookmark stuck out. He read something, keeping his finger on the page. "I'm very pleased to have you visit," he said to Lilly. He glanced at the book again. "I look forward to a very pleasant visit."

"Thank you, Great-Uncle Ernest," said Lilly.

"Just Uncle Ernest will be fine," said her uncle. "I am merely a humble librarian."

Had Uncle Ernest made a joke? Lilly couldn't see his face to tell. He had stooped over to pick up her duffle bag. Suddenly she missed her momma and poppa so

much she could hardly move. She should have gone with them, should have been brave. Now it was too late. Now she was here with Uncle Ernest. At least he was a librarian, not a pirate.

Uncle Ernest headed out of the bus station, and Lilly forced her feet to follow him.

"Uncle Ernest," she asked as they came out into the sunlight, "are there pirates in Mundelaine?"

Uncle Ernest stumbled. "Pirates? No, no, of course not," he said. "There have never been pirates in Mundelaine. Never. Impossible. Unthinkable." The gray handkerchief in his gray suit pocket quivered. He set down her bag, pulled out the handkerchief, and carefully mopped his forehead. Then he neatly folded the handkerchief, tucked it into his suit pocket, arranged the corners, hefted her duffle bag, and set off down the street again.

Lilly hurried to catch up. "What about the man in the station?" she asked.

"What man?" asked Uncle Ernest.

"The one dressed like a pirate."

"Oh. That man. He must have, er, been selling something. Or perhaps on his way to a costume party. Or perhaps all his clothes were at the cleaners and those were the only clothes he had left to wear. I assure you,

Lilly, there have never been nor will there ever be pirates in Mundelaine. This is a quiet town. Certainly not the former site of a pirate school. And even if there were such a school here, no one would ever have wanted to go to it. No one at all."

Uncle Ernest was talking and walking faster and faster. Lilly had to run to keep up with him. She had no reason not to believe him. But who, then, was the strange man in the bus station? Lilly turned back to look. The man was stomping in the opposite direction down the street, his birdcage swinging at the end of his arm. The wind skittered a few leaves after him and gently flapped his ears. The gold earring in one ear caught the sun and threw sparkles of light on the gray concrete walls of the bus station.

Maybe Uncle Ernest was right about no pirates in Mundelaine, but Lilly knew the first thing she would write when she opened her worry book again: *What if Momma and Poppa were attacked by ruthless pirates?*

Uncle Ernest

Uncle Ernest was mostly silent for the rest of the walk to his house. He did point out, with obvious pride, the library where he worked.

Lilly didn't say much either. She was too busy thinking about her momma and poppa. Where were they now? Had they already set sail? Were they safe?

Uncle Ernest's house turned out to be as gray as he was. Gray shingles, gray door, gray trim at the windows where gray curtains hung. The house next door was, if possible, even grayer. A few strips of paint dangled from its bare boards. The porch steps sagged. The roof tilted as though it might slide off. In the backyard a clothesline drooped, and a sign hanging by one nail from the porch railing read FOR RENT.

"Who lives there?" Lilly asked.

Uncle Ernest sniffed. "No one has lived there for quite some time," he said. "I am hopeful that a new owner or tenant will perform the necessary maintenance and repairs to maintain a neat façade."

Lilly followed Uncle Ernest up the gray steps into his house, over the gray carpet, and up the gray stairs.

"This room will be yours," he said. Lilly wasn't surprised to see a gray bedspread and gray blanket on the bed. Uncle Ernest stood in the doorway, paging through the book he still carried. He looked up. "I hope this room meets with your approval," he said.

"It's fine, Uncle Ernest." Lilly didn't care how her room looked. This was just a place to stay until her parents came back for her.

If they came back.

Uncle Ernest was consulting his book again. "I will leave you to unpack and settle in," he said. "Dinner is at six. I, er, I hope you like tofu."

Lilly nodded. What did it matter what she ate? Her fingers itched to open her worry book.

As soon as Uncle Ernest was gone, Lilly wrote page after page until suppertime.

That night, as they ate steamed tofu and mashed

cauliflower, Uncle Ernest flipped through the pages of his book, then looked up at Lilly and asked, "What did you do today?"

Do? He knew what she had done. She had said goodbye to her momma and poppa. She had ridden the bus to Mundelaine. She had met him at the bus station, come to his house, and unpacked her duffle bag. But he looked at her expectantly.

"I rode the bus," said Lilly.

Uncle Ernest looked back at his book, then up again. "Did you have a good time?" he asked.

Uncle Ernest and the book clearly hoped that she did. She guessed finding out that her uncle wasn't a pirate had been good. Lilly nodded.

Uncle Ernest referred to his book again. "And what will you do tomorrow?" he asked.

Hope bloomed suddenly in Lilly's heart. Did Uncle Ernest really want to know? Would he understand if she told him how much time she spent worrying and writing down things in her worry book to keep her momma and poppa safe?

He was glancing at his book again. "Will you have a good time tomorrow?" he asked.

No, Uncle Ernest wouldn't understand. "I'll try," said Lilly.

The book must not have had any more suggestions for conversation. They finished the meal in silence.

That night Lilly finished *Millicent Murray and the Hyena That Didn't Laugh* and started it over again, but rereading the story didn't take her mind off her worries. Tomorrow she would go to the library and find something new to read. Perhaps she could even help Uncle Ernest in the library.

"Help me?" Uncle Ernest said when Lilly brought up the matter the next morning after a breakfast of four-minute eggs and three-minute toast. "At the library? Nobody but the chief librarian is allowed to check books out to people. Or shelve them. Or write numbers on their spines."

"Could I come along anyway and check out some books?" Lilly asked.

"Check out books?" He sounded doubtful. "I suppose you could fill out a library card application and present two forms of identification, and then you would be issued a temporary card with which you might check out two books a week."

Two books a week? Lilly's heart and shoulders sagged. Sometimes, when a new crate of books arrived, she devoured two books a day.

Two books, though, were better than no new books.

"I shall draw you a map to the library," said Uncle Ernest.

"Didn't we pass it walking back from the bus station?" asked Lilly. "I think I can find it again."

"I have found in life that it is wise to have a map wherever you go," said Uncle Ernest. "You never know where you might find yourself otherwise. I've left you a list of chores to do. I hope you don't mind. *A Guide to a Visit from Your Great-Niece*"—he tapped the cover of the thick book—"recommends giving you some responsibilities about the house."

"I don't mind," said Lilly. Anything to make the days and weeks pass faster. Uncle Ernest drew a detailed map, put his gray hat on, and left for the library. Lilly read the list of chores.

Wash dishes.

Dry dishes.

Put dishes away in alphabetical order.

> Cups
>
> Glasses
>
> Plates
>
> Silverware
>
>> Forks
>>
>> Knives
>>
>> Spoons

Chores done, Lilly followed Uncle Ernest's map one block straight down the street to the library.

At the Library

Lilly caught her breath as she stepped through the door. Books. Books and books and books. More books than Lilly had ever seen in her life. Enough to fill hundreds of crates. She inhaled the smell of books and ink and paper. Her fingers ached to pull books off the shelf and leaf through them, read a line here, a page there. She had read about libraries, of course, how you could check books out of them. She had pictured fifty or even a hundred books. Nothing at all like this vast wealth. She could bury herself in reading until her momma and poppa came sailing back to her. Maybe she would even be a librarian when she grew up.

Lilly filled out all the forms in triplicate and handed

them to Uncle Ernest, who reluctantly waived the two forms of identification because, as Lilly pointed out, he knew who she was. Lilly clutched the temporary library card that he handed back to her and wandered past shelf after shelf of books, their spines lined up precisely with the edges of the shelves. How, from all these books, could she choose just two? Maybe she could come to the library every day and sit here and read and read and read. Lilly thought she could live in the library and be almost happy. If only her momma and poppa were here.

But nowhere among all the books did she see the red-and-gold covers for which she was looking.

"Uncle Ernest," Lilly asked, "where are the Millicent Murray mysteries?"

"The what?"

"Mysteries. About Millicent Murray."

"Do you mean fiction?"

Lilly nodded.

"Almost all of the library collection is nonfiction," said Uncle Ernest. "You can't go wrong with facts."

Lilly's heart sagged even further. Uncle Ernest must have seen the look on her face because he said, "It is highly irregular for the chief librarian to leave his desk, but I shall check downstairs in storage. Perhaps there are a few fictional books there."

He carefully locked the library door, turned the Open sign to Closed, and disappeared through a door behind his desk. Lilly wandered back through the rows of books of facts and more facts. She had counted on Millicent Murray to distract her, counted on rereading her way through all thirty-seven volumes (so far) of Millicent's adventures. If she couldn't have Millicent Murray, what would she check out, then? Maybe she could find *A Guide to a Visit with Your Great-Uncle*.

Lilly ran a finger over the titles: *The Life History of Lava. Motes and Mites: The Story of Dust.* Good books, perhaps, but they looked even less interesting than the ones that had come in the crates for her momma and poppa on the life cycles of banana borers.

Momma and Poppa. Where were they now? Were they safe? Had they reached the Shipwreck Islands?

She blinked. There, in front of her, was a book with just those words lettered on the spine: *The Prudent Mariner's Guide to the Shipwreck Islands.*

Fingers shaking, Lilly pulled the book off the shelf. It was a thin volume, barely thick enough to have a title on its spine. She turned to the table of contents: "Hidden Reefs." "Treacherous Tides." "Deadly Currents." Could the Shipwreck Islands be even more dangerous than she had imagined? Heart hammering, Lilly flipped to the first

chapter, "If You Are Going to the Shipwreck Islands." It was a very short chapter, just one word: "DON'T!"

A piece of paper fell out of the book and fluttered to the floor. Lilly picked it up. Someone must have left it in the book—a grocery list, maybe, or a letter. But who would write a letter on such tattered, smudged paper? The ragged edges crumbled under her fingers as Lilly gingerly unfolded the paper. Not a letter, not a list. A crudely drawn map.

The stairs creaked under Uncle Ernest's feet. Without knowing exactly why she did it, Lilly folded the map back up and stuffed it back into the book, clutching it shut to keep the piece of paper from falling out again.

Uncle Ernest held a familiar red-and-gold book. "I did find one in a box of books donated to the library and set aside for the used-book sale," he said. "While I don't recommend it . . ."

"Thank you." Lilly grabbed the book. *Millicent Murray and the Rooster That Didn't Crow*. She had read it before, but she would read it again. "I'm ready to check out now." She had planned to sit in the library and read, but she could almost feel the map pulsing. It wasn't the kind of thing Uncle Ernest would have allowed in the library if he knew it was there.

She held her breath while he checked out the books.

Would the map fall out? Would Uncle Ernest con-fiscate it?

But the map stayed hidden inside. All the way home she clutched the book. When she got up the stairs to her room, she spread the map out on her gray bedspread. There were odd lines and squiggles, an arrow pointing to a circle with lines radiating out in four directions. And in one corner of the map by a big X, the rambling printing read *Heer be tresur.*

Mysterious Laundry

Lilly pored over the map until it felt burned onto the insides of her eyelids. Was this place the Shipwreck Islands? Except for the printing staggering across the one corner, there were no other words. Just cryptic symbols. What was that lopsided circle with an X over it? Or was it just dirt? Was the map part of the book or just tucked into it?

The book itself was not much more help. Although the chapters after chapter 1 were longer, Lilly found little hard information in them. No one, it seemed (according to *The Guide*), had ever gone to the Shipwreck Islands and returned to tell about them. Then who had written the book? Everything in the book seemed to be rumors, guesses, wild stories. Were there really man-eating palm trees? Sea serpents? Giant sea gulls? Lilly didn't think so, but just the thought of those perils was enough to make her slam the book shut time after time and write in her worry book. She always went back to *The Prudent Mariner's Guide to the Shipwreck Islands*, though. Better to know the worst that could happen so she could worry against it.

Skreee-kee-ree.

Lilly ran from the room, down the stairs, and out the door to see what the squalling was all about. Perched on a tree was a sea gull, a thin strip of paper wrapped around its leg.

Momma and Poppa! Lilly's fingers shook as she untied the string that held the note to the sea gull's leg and unrolled the paper. Were they all right?

The tiny printing read:

Lovely sailing. Miss you much.
Love, Momma and Poppa

And in even tinier printing underneath:

P.S. Please feed the gull.

Clutching the paper to her chest, Lilly ran into the house again and searched Uncle Ernest's refrigerator. Tofu casserole and a tin of sardines. She grabbed them both and hurried back outside. The sea gull turned up its beak at the casserole but gobbled down the sardines, eyeballs and all, while Lilly wrote her own note:

Miss you A LOT. Am being good as gold. Love, Lilly
Then she tied it to the sea gull's leg and watched the bird flap away.

She carried the strip of paper upstairs and pressed it carefully in her worry book. Momma and Poppa were safe. For now. And they still loved her.

When Lilly had finally read all of *The Prudent Mariner's Guide to the Shipwreck Islands* and written down every worry she could think of, she ran back down the street to the library. Maybe she could find some other book on the Shipwrecks, one that wasn't so full of disastrous possibilities.

Uncle Ernest looked up, startled, as she banged in through the door. "I'm afraid you can't check any more books out until your card is processed, Lilly," he told her.

"I just want to look around," Lilly said. She felt his anxious eyes on her back as she scoured the shelves again.

Lilly scanned title after title about earthworms as pets, washtub-bass tuning, the life cycle of dandelions.

But nowhere did she find anything else on the Shipwreck Islands.

The whole time, Uncle Ernest's wary gaze followed her around. Did he think she would scribble in a book? Steal one? Was that what a librarian did all day, sit like a prison guard? Maybe she didn't want to be a librarian after all.

And oddly, though she spent the whole afternoon searching the shelves, no one else came into the library.

"Is the library always so quiet?" she asked Uncle Ernest at dinner that night. "Where is everyone?"

Uncle Ernest carefully cut his tofu casserole into identical pieces. He did not meet her eyes. Odder still, he did not leaf through *A Guide to a Visit from Your Great-Niece* by his elbow.

"Well," he said, "the children are all off to camps in the summer."

"All of them?"

"It is a long tradition in Mundelaine for parents to send their children off to camps each summer to keep them safe from idle influences. I myself went to future librarians' camp many years ago, although if I could have chosen the camp . . ." A faraway look blew across Uncle Ernest's face. He placed a bite of casserole in his mouth. When he had chewed and swallowed, he looked up at Lilly. "And what did you do today?" he asked. "Did you have a good time?"

Day followed day. Each morning Lilly did the list of chores Uncle Ernest left. She read and reread her two Millicent Murray books. She filled up one worry book and started another. At night Uncle Ernest asked, "How was your day?" Every night Lilly said the same thing: "Fine." The gray days leaked into one another. Even the idea of getting a library card didn't brighten Lilly's thoughts. What would she check out? *The A to Z of Refrigerator Repair*? To her short list of things she didn't want to be, Lilly had already added "librarian in Mundelaine."

The only things that changed each day were what kind of tofu dish they ate for dinner and the messages that came by homing sea gull. Each time a sea gull arrived, Lilly carefully unwrapped the paper wound around its leg, read it, and pressed it between the pages of her worry book.

Saw flying fish today. Love, Momma and Poppa

Winds strong and steady. Making good time. Love, Momma and Poppa

Becalmed but doing fine. Love, Momma and Poppa

Winds picking up. Landfall tomorrow. Love, Momma and Poppa

Every day Lilly carefully wrote back: *Am being good as gold. Love, Lilly*

Then she wrote in her worry book.

What if flying fish tore holes in the sails?

What if the winds blew Momma and Poppa off course to Antarctica?

What if they were becalmed forever in a wide Sargasso Sea?

One morning when Lilly went into the backyard to write in her worry book and read and wait for the day's message by homing sea gull, color dazzled her eyes. The dreary house next door was still shuttered tight, but the clothesline no longer hung empty. A peacock-blue shawl with fuchsia fringe billowed. A red skirt with yellow lace ballooned. Turquoise bloomers danced. A scarlet shirt with lace cuffs shimmied. Something that looked suspiciously like a sword belt swayed gently back and forth, and two eye patches, one regular size and one tiny, fluttered in the wind.

The Stranger

L illy couldn't tear her eyes off the laundry. It glowed in the sunshine. Who could own such strange and glorious clothes? Lilly leaned on the fence, staring and staring. While she stared, a stranger slunk along the alley and stopped by a tree in the backyard of the house next door.

His barrel of a body was squeezed into a shiny brown suit, his hat was jammed low on his head, and his black beard bristled. He lugged a suitcase with *BRUSSHES* lettered crudely on the side. There was something familiar about him. Was this the new neighbor?

The stranger peered closely at the trunk of a tree growing at the edge of the yard. He reached out a finger (even from a distance, Lilly could see that it was large and hairy) and traced something on the trunk. He spied Lilly watching him, wrestled a smile onto his face and said in a syrupy voice, "Hello, little girl. Is your neighbor to home?"

Lilly had never, as far as she remembered, been called "little girl." She didn't like it now.

"I'm a brush salesman, I am," the stranger went on. "Mebbe yer neighbor might be needing some brushes for, er, for her laundry." He cocked his head at the clothesline. His ears waved like washcloths hung out to dry.

"I don't know," Lilly said. Which was true. She didn't even know who lived in the house.

"What about yer mum and dad, then?" the stranger asked. "Are they to home? Might be they know summat about yer neighbor?"

Lilly knew better than to tell a stranger, any stranger, that she was home alone. But how could she tell a lie and still be good as gold?

"My uncle Ernest is working and can't be disturbed," said Lilly. This wasn't exactly a lie. Lilly suspected that Uncle Ernest hated to be disturbed by anything, even people wanting to check out books. Especially people wanting to check out books. "My momma and poppa are away," she added. How much of the truth should she tell? In *Millicent Murray and the Crow That Didn't Caw*, Millicent Murray had told almost all the truth, which had been even better than a lie because it sounded so believable. When she had claimed to be a crow tamer, Millicent just hadn't mentioned that she had come to steal the crows back from the crow thieves.

"My momma and poppa are in the Shipwreck Islands," Lilly added.

The stranger's smile slid off his face. "Oh, they are, are they?" he snarled. "And what might they be doing there? Don't jist happen to have a map, do they? Not searching for anything, are they? Not doing any digging now, are they?"

Were they digging? Had they even arrived yet? Lilly wouldn't know until the daily sea gull arrived. Whatever Lilly's momma and poppa were doing, they were doing it there, and she was here, without them. Besides, she had already told this stranger much more than he needed to know.

"I have to go now," she said. "I think my uncle is calling me." That wasn't exactly a lie either. Uncle Ernest might be at the library calling her. Not likely, but not necessarily a lie.

A gust of wind rustled the tree leaves and snatched

the stranger's hat off his head. He grabbed for the hat, and dropped his suitcase. It bounced, the latch broke open, and out rolled a birdcage. Not a brush in sight.

The sun shone through the stranger's ears so that they looked like giant pink seashells. An earring gleamed in one ear. The stranger snatched up his birdcage and crammed it back into the suitcase, smashed his hat back on his head, and stomped away.

And now Lilly knew where she had seen the stranger before. He had been waiting in the Mundelaine bus station. Only then he had looked like a pirate.

The laundry flapped on the line. The tree whispered in the wind. What had been so interesting on that tree to the brush-salesman pirate? With a glance at the shuttered windows of the dilapidated house, Lilly clambered over the fence, between the dancing clothes, and over to the tree. Just an ordinary tree. The breeze gusted again, and a crack of sunlight shot between the branches onto the bark. Bare wood gleamed. Lilly leaned closer. Something was carved in the bark of the tree. Something that looked like a lopsided circle with an X below it. Lilly reached out a finger and traced the carving. She had seen this circle before, with an X just like this one. She had seen the marks scratched onto the corner of the map in the

book on the table by her bed. Not a circle at all, she could see now, and the X was below it, not above. She had been looking at it upside down. The squiggle was a skull, with crossed bones underneath.

The House
Next Door

And now Lilly had a new worry. She opened her worry
book and scribbled, *What if a pirate disguised as
a brush salesman wants to sell brushes that are really
a birdcage to a new neighbor, and that pirate knows
about the Shipwreck Islands and . . .* And what? Lilly
didn't even know how to finish that sentence. She didn't
even know precisely what she needed to worry about to
protect her momma and poppa.

Did the new neighbor know about the Shipwreck
Islands, too? Maybe she could tell Lilly about them. And
Lilly could warn her about the pirate in disguise as a

brush salesman, or maybe the brush salesman disguised as a pirate. Whoever he was, Lilly was sure he was up to no good.

What would Millicent Murray do? She would march right up to the neighbor's door and knock. She might find a disguise of her own if she didn't want to be recognized, maybe go as a traveling sock mender, but go she would. And so would Lilly. She would do it for her momma and poppa's sake. Millicent Murray always said that desperate situations demanded desperate actions, and at the moment Lilly was feeling a little desperate.

Heart pounding, Lilly climbed the neighbor's rickety stairs, careful to avoid the rotted hole at the edge of the next-to-top step. The porch floor creaked under her. Her hand came up, hesitated in front of the warped wood and peeling paint. The raggedy curtain hung behind the cracked glass. She tapped on the front door. No one answered.

Lilly snatched her hand away. What had she done? What would she say that wouldn't sound foolish? Good, no one was coming. She could go back to Uncle Ernest's and write in her worry book and wait until her momma and poppa came safely back and wrapped her in their arms.

The door snicked open. From inside the dark shuttered house a voice simpered, "Yes, dearie?" A salty smell drifted through the open door.

Another voice squawked, "Make her walk the plank! *Awk! Cluck!*"

"Pay no attention to me chicken," simpered the first voice.

"I'm sorry to bother you, Miss . . . ," Lilly stammered.

"It's Missus, dearie. Mrs. Teagarden. Jist a simple housewife and her simple chicken."

"*Awk! Cluck!*"

"Mrs. Teagarden, well, someone . . . someone in disguise . . ."

A hand snaked out through the crack in the door and grasped Lilly's arm. A surprisingly strong hand. Was that a tattoo on the wrist?

"Disguises, is it? Seen through mine, have ye?" the voice hissed, and there was nothing simpering about it now.

The hand dragged Lilly into the darkness of the house. The door slammed shut behind her.

Lilly's heart beat wildly. In the dusty light falling through the cracks in the shutters, she could just make out the woman gripping her wrist, a woman with a mop of wild white hair, a frilly pink dress with an apron tied crooked at her waist, and fluffy green slippers. A bird sat on her shoulder, a bird that looked like a parrot wearing a feather duster.

"*Awk!* Keelhaul her! *Cluck!*" the bird squawked.

"Hush, chickie," Mrs. Teagarden said. "How would we keelhaul her when we haven't a boat or a keel to haul her under?"

Mrs. Teagarden dragged Lilly deeper into the dim house and shoved her down into a sheet-covered chair. Dust rose in clouds. Lilly coughed. "Here now, where are me manners?" said Mrs. Teagarden. "Would ye be wanting a drop to drink, dearie? Ye're a mite young for rumfustian, but I was jist sitting down to a glass of lemonade. Then ye kin tell me what ye have to say."

Lilly shook her head and coughed again. Never, never drink anything in a strange house with a strange person. Millicent Murray knew that, and so did Lilly.

But Mrs. Teagarden had already turned away to a sheet-covered table with a pitcher and glasses on it. She poured two glasses and handed one to Lilly.

The glass looked cool and inviting. Just a little sip wouldn't hurt. Just to clear her aching, raspy throat so she could explain and then leave. Lilly took the tiniest

sip she could manage. Cool and tart, the liquid slipped down her throat.

Mrs. Teagarden drew a green glass bottle from the front of her dress and poured a few drops from it into her own glass. The lemonade sputtered and fizzed. She settled back into a chair, dust rising around her, and took a long drink. "Ah, lemons," she sighed. "The sailor's friend. Keeps a body from getting all scurvilous. Now down to business. How did ye see through me disguise?"

"But I didn't," said Lilly. Relief flooded through her. This was all a mistake. She would explain, and Mrs. Teagarden would let her go. "I wanted to warn you about someone else in disguise. He was creeping into your backyard and asking questions about you. He said he was a brush salesman, but all he had in his brush suitcase was a birdcage—"

"*Awk!* Mayday!" screamed the parrot in the feather duster. "Abandon ship! Abandon ship!"

"Hush yer beak!" snapped Mrs. Teagarden. She turned back to Lilly. Her eyes glittered dangerously. "Did he have a bushy black beard and sails for ears?" asked Mrs. Teagarden.

Lilly nodded.

"Blackheart the pirate, curse his ears," Mrs.

Teagarden growled. She banged her glass down on a dusty end table. "And I know what he's after."

"What?" Lilly asked in spite of herself.

"Why, what every pirate worth his salt is after, dearie. The treasure of William Barnacle."

The Pirate's Oath

Lilly knew what she should do next: run as fast as she could away from this crazy lady and her crazy bird. What Lilly did next surprised even herself. She leaned forward in her chair and said, "William who?"

"William Barnacle," said Mrs. Teagarden. "Only the greatest pirate that ever sailed the six seas. Or is it seven? Before he vanished into the Shipwreck Islands."

The Shipwrecks! "Do you know about them?" asked Lilly. "Can you tell me everything you know?"

"Well, could be I know, and could be I'd tell ye, but only on one condition."

"What?"

"Well, dearie, since it's secret pirate business I'd be telling ye, and since ye already know more than is good for ye about me disguise, ye'll jist have to take the pirate's oath and become a pirate yerself."

Lilly carefully set her glass on the table and stood up. "I have to go now," she said, her voice wobbly.

But Mrs. Teagarden was standing, too, and her hand was once again wrapped around Lilly's wrist, tight as a manacle.

"Aye, it's the pirate's oath for ye, dearie," Mrs. Teagarden said. "Whither ye want to or no. There's no getting out of it."

"*Awk! Squawk!* Hang her from the yardarm!"

Lilly tugged to free her wrist. Pirates robbed people. Pirates attacked ships with pistols and cutlasses. Pirates swore and swashbuckled and made people walk the plank. Pirates weren't good as gold waiting for their mommas and poppas to come back to them. If she could just get away, she would bolt out the door, across the lawn, and all the way to the library, where Uncle Ernest was probably lining up the edges of books on their shelves.

But then what? Would Uncle Ernest believe Lilly if she babbled about pirates? Would he have to check in

A Guide to a Visit from Your Great-Niece to see if it mentioned pirate neighbors? What if it didn't? What would he do?

Mrs. Teagarden tightened her iron grip. "First I must warn ye—" Mrs. Teagarden fixed Lilly with a fierce eye, while the parrot-disguised-as-a-chicken fixed Lilly with a beady eye—"once ye take the oath, there's no breaking it. Hornswoggler Pete broke the oath, and he was eaten by sharks. Fearsome Fernando only thought about breaking the oath, and he was carried off by a flock of frigate birds."

Mrs. Teagarden smiled snarkily. Maybe she was just crazy. Maybe, just maybe, if Lilly only pretended to be a pirate, Mrs. Teagarden would tell her everything Lilly needed to know about the Shipwrecks and Lilly could go back to Uncle Ernest's and work on these new worries to keep Momma and Poppa safe and never knock on a stranger's door again.

What would Millicent Murray do?

Lilly clenched her fists so tight her fingernails dug into her palms. "I'll take the oath," she said.

Mrs. Teagarden drew herself up tall. Even the parrot in the feather-duster wig loomed larger and more sinister. "Repeat after me: 'By all the gold and pirates' bones, I swear to follow the pirate code.'"

"The pirate code?" Just what was she swearing to?

"The usual," said Mrs. Teagarden. "Distribution of loot by shares, captain's word is law unless another captain is elected, lights out by eight, no sharing pirate secrets, that sort of thing."

Lights-out at Uncle Ernest's was ten o'clock sharp. Her momma and poppa never even had lights-out. They had all stayed up reading as late as they pleased.

Lilly swallowed a lump and lifted her chin. "'By all the gold and pirates' bones, I swear to follow the pirates' code.'"

"'Or swim forever in Davy Jones's Locker.'"

"'Or swim forever in Davy Jones's Locker,'" said Lilly. "What's Davy Jones's Locker?"

"The bottom of the sea." Mrs. Teagarden sniffed and swiped at her eyes, letting loose of Lilly's wrist. "Always chokes me up, that does, dearie."

Now, if ever, was Lilly's chance to escape while Mrs. Teagarden blew her nose in a black bandanna. But something held Lilly there. Maybe it was the little shift she had felt in her chest when she had taken the oath. Maybe it was the chance to learn more about the Shipwrecks. Maybe there really had been something in the lemonade she had drunk. Maybe all those things together.

Whatever it was, Lilly had taken the oath. She had earned the right to hear whatever Mrs. Teagarden had to say about the Shipwreck Islands and William Barnacle.

Lilly sat back down in her chair.

Millicent Murray would have been proud.

The Tale of
William Barnacle

As I was saying, dearie." Mrs. Teagarden paused to take a long sip from her lemonade. "William Barnacle was the best pirate ever to sail the seas, however many there are. Used to be William the scholar, he did. Spent all his time doing research at the library until he was kidnapped by a pirate crew. Some folks say book learning is dangerous, and in William's case it's true. His arms were piled so high with books he was taking back to the library that he nivver saw the pirates till they grabbed him. The pirates almost didn't take William, he was so puny, but they needed someone to swab the decks and they had a tide to catch."

Lilly shuddered. Having just been grabbed herself, she knew how William must have felt.

"Hung on to those books like barnacles, he did," Mrs. Teagarden went on, "which is how he got his name. Kicked up such a ruckus, the pirates took the books along, too, jist to shut William up. And all he did for the longest time was fret about getting back to pay his library fines. But after a while he began to change. His arms grew stronger from deck swabbing and cutlass polishing, and the sea air steadied his legs. The biggest change, though, was that William discovered a dark and dusty corner of his heart that loved pirating. It was a small corner, mind ye, but a fierce and swashbuckling one. After that, he was first over the rail when they captured a ship, and whenever sailors heard his terrible teeth-crunching oaths, they threw down their swords and begged to surrender."

"What were the oaths?" Lilly asked in spite of herself.

Mrs. Teagarden considered Lilly. "Ye're a mite young for the likes of his oaths," she said. "But seeing as how ye're a pirate now, I'll tell ye a couple of the milder ones." She sat up tall in her chair and shouted, "'By the square of the hypotenuse! Ontogeny recapitulates phylogeny! $E = mc$ squared!'"

Lilly shivered.

"*Awk!* Surrender or die! *Cluck!*" squawked the parrot.

"And whenivver the pirates captured a ship," Mrs. Teagarden said, settling back in her chair, "William took all the books he could lay his hands on as his share of the booty. The other pirates didn't mind. More treasure for them to share, and most of the pirates couldn't read one letter from another."

Lilly couldn't imagine not being able to read. All those books, all those words, closed and locked up and waiting. No Millicent Murray. No notes from her momma and poppa. No chance to read and imagine any of the things Lilly might be besides a scientist.

"William changed all that, too," Mrs. Teagarden went on. "On dead-calm days when not a whiff of wind stirred the sails, William held school, and every man jack of the pirates discovered a dark and dusty corner of his heart that loved learning. Soon every hand on William's ship could spell *rumfustian* faster than he could guzzle down a bottle of it."

Mrs. Teagarden pulled the green glass bottle out of her dress and added a few more fizzing drops to her lemonade. "The other pirates elected William captain, and a fine captain he was, too, until he disappeared in the Shipwreck Islands," Mrs. Teagarden said.

Lilly's fingers felt cold. Here was a terrible new worry. What if her momma and poppa were captured by William Barnacle? "Is he still in the Shipwreck Islands?" she asked.

"Marooned! Marooned! *Awk!*"

"Hush, chickie," said Mrs. Teagarden. She took a sip from her glass. "Some folks say he sailed into those islands and nivver sailed out. Some say he buried his share of the treasure there to make more room on his ship for his books. Some say he went down on the reefs with all hands. And some folks think the only one who knows what happened is his parrot, Aristotle, who turned up one day at a rummage sale for the Pirates' Relief Fund."

Lilly looked at the parrot disguised with a feather duster. "Is this . . . ?" It couldn't be. It was too impossible.

Mrs. Teagarden nodded. "Right ye are," she said. "This is Aristotle."

Kee-ree-kee-kee-skrree-skreee-skreee! A cacophony of wild calls set the dust motes in the air shivering.

"We're under attack!" shouted Mrs. Teagarden. She grabbed up a cutlass and raced for the back door, yanking it open. "Well, shiver me timbers!" Mrs. Teagarden exclaimed.

Careful of the cutlass in Mrs. Teagarden's grip, Lilly crept out the door after her.

The tree in Uncle Ernest's backyard was covered in sea gulls.

A Tree Full of Birds

"What in blimey blazes are they doing here?" asked Mrs. Teagarden.

Lilly gulped. "My momma and poppa are sailing," she said. "They took the sea gulls so they could write every day. But why are all the sea gulls here at once?"

Mrs. Teagarden looked down at Lilly. Was that pity on her face?

A piece of paper dangled from the leg of one sea gull. Lilly untied the paper and unrolled it.

Have hit reef, sinkin

Lilly stared at the unfinished word. Her knees wobbled.

Mrs. Teagarden patted her roughly. "Shipwreck, sure as seashells," said Mrs. Teagarden. "Loosed from their cages all at once."

"We have to tell someone so they can go and rescue them," Lilly cried. "Uncle Ernest or, or . . ."

Mrs. Teagarden was shaking her head. "No, dearie. Ye go blabbing to anyone about heading for the Shipwrecks, and Blackheart's bound to hear what we're about, and ye don't want him heading there, too. Blackheart might think yer parents was after William Barnacle's treasure, jist like he is, and he wouldn't take kindly to finding them there. Besides, ye're a pirate now, and a pirate looks after her own. Ye'll jist have to go to the rescue yerself. But nivver ye worry. I'll be coming along. Pirates help pirates, that's what the code says. Unless, of course, a pirate's after yer gold. Then it's every man jack for hisself."

Gold! Lilly had tried to be good as gold, really she had, and just look what had happened.

"It jist so happens I've got business in the Shipwrecks meself," said Mrs. Teagarden.

"I thought no one knew how to find them," said Lilly. "That's what the book I was reading about the Shipwreck Islands said."

Mrs. Teagarden winked. "There's some what knows

and some what don't," she said. "And besides, there's always the chance Aristotle can find our way there. Lucky for ye that ye took the oath and can come along with me. So what do ye say, dearie? Are ye out or are ye in?"

Lilly quailed. How could she sail over the great dark, heaving ocean, even to save her dear momma and poppa? Shouldn't somebody else take care of it?

But what if Lilly and Mrs. Teagarden were her parents' only hope?

What would Millicent Murray do?

Millicent Murray would go, of course. She would find Lilly's momma and poppa and bring them home safe.

Well, she had taken the pirate's oath. Maybe, just maybe she could force herself to get on a boat and sail. Lilly straightened her shoulders. Momma and Poppa needed her.

"I'll go," she said. "But what should I tell Uncle Ernest?"

"Best not to tell him at all, unless he's a dab hand at sailing. We could always use another mate."

Lilly tried to imagine Uncle Ernest on board a ship. His gray hat stayed firmly on his head. His hair refused to blow in the wind.

"I don't think he's a sailor," Lilly said.

"Ye'll have to sneak away in disguise, then," said Mrs. Teagarden. "Be ready at eight bells. And bring that book ye were talking about. Happen it might have a chart of the Shipwrecks."

"Shipwreck Islands! Bring her about! *Awk!*"

"What kind of chart?" Lilly asked.

"That's what we sea salts calls a map, dearie," Mrs. Teagarden said. "Jist bring it along. Ye nivver know when a book might come in handy."

"I'll send Momma and Poppa a note back," Lilly said. Momma and Poppa had to be safe. They would get the note. They would read it. They would know Lilly was on her way.

Coming. Love, Lilly, she wrote on the back of the paper and wrapped it back around the skinny leg of one of the gulls. A gust shook the tree. The sea gulls lifted into the air and flapped away.

Lilly blinked back tears. Now there was nothing she could do but find a disguise and wait until eight bells, whenever that meant, to sneak away. To sea.

Jump!

Luckily eight bells turned out to be after dark. Lilly figured that out by looking in *The Prudent Mariner's Guide to the Shipwreck Islands*. In the dark her disguise didn't matter so much. Lilly had been hard put to find anything at Uncle Ernest's that would work as a disguise. Finally she draped a gray sheet over herself. If she drifted slowly along, maybe she could pass for a cloud or a fogbank. She couldn't see herself in the mirror through the sheet to be certain.

In the drawer of Uncle Ernest's desk labeled S–V, Lilly found a pair of scissors. Cutting eyeholes in the sheet surely wasn't being good as gold, but neither was running away. *Snip, snip.* Lilly snipped two eyeholes in her disguise.

After dinner ("How was your day?" "Fine, Uncle Ernest, how was yours?" "Satisfactory."), Lilly sat with her worry book open in her lap, but her worries loomed so big that she didn't know where to start. Who knew what lay ahead? How could she even guess what to worry about? Maybe so many worries were a kind of worry overload. She had just written *What if* and was wondering what to write next when something flapped at the window. Aristotle, minus the feather duster, with an eye patch over one eye and a round plastic cap on his head, hovered outside the glass, then flapped away. It must be almost eight bells. Uncle Ernest had already brushed his teeth, called good-night, turned out his light, and begun to snore softly as he did every night at exactly five minutes after ten.

Lilly stuffed *The Prudent Mariner's Guide to the Shipwreck Islands*—with the treasure map carefully folded inside—into the front of her shirt, added her two Millicent Murray books, tucked in her worry book—where she had carefully pressed all the notes from her momma and poppa—and threw on her sheet. Looking like a solid fogbank, Lilly made her way downstairs and out the door. Luckily Uncle Ernest's door hinges didn't squeak. He should sleep soundly until 5:59 the next morning, when he would wake up and find the note Lilly had left on her pillow.

Gone to find Momma and Poppa lost at sea.

Sincerely, Lilly

PS: I will buy you another sheet and pay my library fines when I come back.

If she came back.

Lilly crept onto the porch next door and knocked softly. Mrs. Teagarden's door opened and a voice complained, "Now look at all this fog that's rolled in."

"It's me," Lilly whispered, "in disguise."

"Oh! Good disguise," Mrs. Teagarden whispered back. She dragged a cart piled with clothes out onto the porch. Mrs. Teagarden still had on the pink dress and frilly apron, only now she wore a shawl wrapped around her shoulders, heavy boots on her feet, a sword belt with a sword buckled on, and an eye patch over one eye. "And I'm jist a simple housewife off to do me laundry."

Aristotle, in his eye patch with the cap of a laundry-detergent bottle on his head, was perched on the cart. "Ring around the collar! Yo ho ho!" he squawked.

"He's the detergent," Mrs. Teagarden whispered. "Lucky there's an all-night Laundromat by the pier so we don't look suspicious." She wrestled the cart down the steps.

Behind her, the wind seized the door, flung it wide, then whammed it shut. A light came on in Uncle Ernest's house.

"Shake out yer sails, dearie," Mrs. Teagarden whispered.

Lilly guessed that meant to hurry. She hurried, doing her best to drift. Mrs. Teagarden sang, "Rub a dub, off for a scrub." The cart wheels clanked. Aristotle yo-ho-hoed. They were almost to the pier when Lilly heard another noise above the singing and yo-ho-hoing and clanking. Was that footsteps behind them?

She turned to look, but the eyeholes twisted and all she could see was the inside of the sheet. Someone grabbed Lilly from behind. A big black boot with silver buckles poked under the edge of the sheet. Lilly's heart jumped.

"Gotcha," a voice snarled. "Hand over that blasted bird, or I'll run through yer fogbank here with me cutlass."

Lilly heard a sound like a sword being pulled out of a sword belt.

"Unhand that fogbank, Blackheart!" Mrs. Teagarden shouted.

Lilly flailed, but her arms were held fast. *The Prudent Mariner's Guide to the Shipwreck Islands* slipped out of her shirt and crashed on the boot.

"Yeouch! Blast and blunderation!" the voice yelped.

The hands let Lilly loose. She flung off the sheet. Mrs. Teagarden was swinging her sword wildly, but she didn't appear to be hitting anything. Someone tangled in a sheet hopped on one foot, cursing.

"Run!" shouted Mrs. Teagarden. She pelted down the dock, cart clanking. Lilly raced after.

"Here's a likely one." Mrs. Teagarden tossed her laundry bundle on board a small boat and hopped over the side. Aristotle, still wearing his detergent bottle cap, flapped to the mast.

"Isn't this your boat?" Lilly asked from the dock.

"It is now." Mrs. Teagarden pulled hard on a rope, and suddenly a sail was flapping up the mast.

"I can't steal a boat," Lilly wailed.

"Ye're a pirate now, ain't ye? This is what pirates do. Untie that line and push us away from the dock, then jump on. Look lively, now."

"Shake a leg! *Awk!*"

A rope stretched from the boat to the dock. Lilly struggled to untie it. The coarse fibers pricked her palms. Maybe this whole rescue plan wasn't such a good idea

82

after all. Cutting holes in sheets was one thing. Stealing a sailboat was another. Lilly still had time to return to Uncle Ernest's, creep up the stairs, and climb back in bed. But then who would rescue Momma and Poppa? Would Mrs. Teagarden go on her own?

The boat began to move slowly away from the pier. The boards of the dock shook under Lilly's feet. Blackheart, freed from the sheet, thundered down the pier toward her.

Lilly looked down. In the gap between boat and pier, the sea lapped.

"Jump on!" cried Mrs. Teagarden.

The sails caught the wind. The gap widened.

Blackheart thundered closer. Someone in gray pajamas loped after him. Still Lilly hesitated.

Between the boat and the dock, the sea gurgled and growled.

"Lilly! Wait!" cried Uncle Ernest.

"I've got ye now!" shouted Blackheart.

"JUMP!" cried Mrs. Teagarden.

Her momma and poppa needed her.

Lilly jumped.

Heave Ho!

The boat deck tilted under Lilly's feet. She teetered. The black water yawned beneath her.

Mrs. Teagarden grabbed Lilly's arm and yanked her down. Lilly plopped in the bottom of the boat, the sail snapping and flapping above her.

"Bring her about!" squawked Aristotle. "Twenty degrees to port. *Awk!*"

"Twenty degrees it is," agreed Mrs. Teagarden. "As good a direction as any." She pushed a long stick that disappeared over the end of the little boat to one side.

Whoomp! Wind caught the sails. The boat leaped forward and careened out of the harbor. The side of the boat Lilly was on tilted perilously close to the dark, rolling waves. Lilly whimpered and scrambled to the side of the boat that rode high above the water.

Shouts followed them, but the wind wrapped around the words, and the shouts grew fainter and fainter. The *woosh, woosh* of waves filled her ears. That, and another sound. Mrs. Teagarden was laughing. Moonlight glinted off her teeth.

"Ah, the wind in yer sails, the waves smacking yer bow. What could be better? Where shall we sail, then, dearie?"

Mrs. Teagarden had forgotten! She had tricked Lilly onto the boat to sail the world doing dastardly pirate deeds. Lilly's momma and poppa would perish, because no one else knew they were shipwrecked. And it would be all Lilly's fault for trusting a pirate.

"The Shipwreck Islands," Lilly gasped. "To rescue my parents."

"Oh, right ye are. I was carried away for a moment, I was, feeling the salt air in me face. Nothing I like better than a boat under me feet. Don't ye worry, dearie. Yer parents'll be right as rain. The Shipwrecks it is."

"Ready about. *Awk! Cluck!*" squawked Aristotle.

"Ready about. Hard alee," said Mrs. Teagarden. "We're changing directions, dearie." The sails flapped, caught the wind, and the high side of the boat where

Lilly clung was suddenly the low side. She whimpered and clawed her way back to the other side.

When the boat and her breath had steadied a bit, Lilly looked around. "Where are the life jackets?" she asked.

"Nivver needed one yet," said Mrs. Teagarden. "And I've sunk many a boat. If we go down, jist grab on to the nearest thing that floats by." She squinted up at the sails and pulled on another rope. "Lucky the wind's coming up. Nothing like a little night sailing to get the blood going."

Lilly's blood wasn't moving, but her stomach suddenly was. Up and down, up and down, up, up, up . . .

Lilly leaned over the high side of the boat.

"Downwind!" shouted Mrs. Teagarden. She seized Lilly and tossed her back to the low side of the boat. The glittering waves rose and fell inches from Lilly's nose. Lilly tried to drag herself back to the high side, but Mrs. Teagarden's arm held her down. Was she trying to drown Lilly?

"Never heave on the windward side," Mrs. Teagarden roared. "That's the side the wind's coming over. Jist blows it back on yer shipmates, and then they toss you over, too. Barfing Bill was tossed overboard so often he learned to swim well enough to win the Pirates'

Olympics. Always toss yer cookies on the leeward side so the wind blows them away. "

Lilly hadn't eaten any cookies for dinner. She leaned over the side of the boat and tossed her mashed turnips and tofu into the water.

"*Awk! Cluck!* Yuck!" squawked Aristotle.

"Ye'll feel yer sea legs in a bit," said Mrs. Teagarden. Lilly didn't care about her sea legs. What she wanted was land legs, legs planted on dry land. Solid land. Land that didn't go up and down and up and down and up and up . . .

Lilly flung herself over the back edge of the boat and heaved again. As she hung head down, she could make out the name of the boat painted on the chipped and weathered side: *Last Chance.*

Was it her last chance, too? Lilly stared down into the black waves, into the eyes of the sea that had once tried to steal her momma and poppa away. She had been little then, no more than three, playing in the sand while her parents crouched down studying beach-bottle beetles. A wave had arched over them, green and wild. She had been too scared even to scream a warning, and the wave had pulled them into the sea, tumbled them in glassy green water before throwing them back onto the beach again. Lilly had screamed then, screamed and screamed no matter how much they tried to comfort her. She had never trusted water again.

The night went by in a blur. Aristotle clucked directions. Mrs. Teagarden stood, feet planted, swaying with the boat. Every so often she adjusted some rope or other, and the sails shifted. Lilly didn't care which way they went. Her stomach felt empty down to her toenails, but still she heaved again and again.

Heaving over the edge of the boat, Lilly saw many amazing things. The water sparkled like yellow fireflies. Flying fish leaped. Once, something dark broke the water in an arc alongside her. Lilly was too weary even to shriek. Almost too weary to worry.

"Dolphin," said Mrs. Teagarden. "Good luck for sailors."

The only good luck Lilly could imagine was finding firm land, land that didn't move an inch. And wherever it was, even a tiny rock in the middle of the ocean, even a speck of a rock, Lilly would never leave it again. And she would throw *The Prudent Mariner's Guide to the Shipwreck Islands* as far into the ocean as she could and let the fish read it.

Lilly curled up exhausted in the bottom of the boat, too sick even to take out her worry book and write in it. Sometime in the night, Lilly thought she heard Mrs.

Teagarden singing. It sounded like a lullaby. By that time, everything around Lilly seemed dreamlike. Bad-dreamlike. What was there to sing about? Nothing.

At last the sky lightened. Lilly pulled herself up, a wrung-out rag, and looked around.

Gray water. Gray sky. An Uncle Ernest sort of day. Lilly wished with all her heart that she were sitting down to breakfast in Uncle Ernest's gray house with safe, gray Uncle Ernest eating a gray breakfast. Not that she would eat anything. Lilly's stomach didn't want to eat ever again.

"Daylight soon," Mrs. Teagarden said. "I been following that blasted bird's directions, but I reckon he doesn't really know what he's squawking about. Feels like we been going in circles. Best have a look at yer book and see where we've got to."

Lilly fumbled in her shirt. Out came her worry book. Now that it was light, now that she wasn't tossing any more cookies, she could write down all her worries so they wouldn't come true. And she would add one more job to her list of things she didn't want to be when she grew up: sailor.

Out came *Millicent Murray and the Hyena That Didn't Laugh. Millicent Murray and the Rooster That Didn't Crow.*

Lilly reached deeper into her shirt. No more books. Lilly dimly remembered an arm grabbing her, a boot, a book falling. Not only the book was gone, but the treasure map tucked inside as well. And all her notes from her momma and poppa.

She looked up at Mrs. Teagarden. "I don't have it," she said in a small voice. "It fell out."

Mrs. Teagarden's eyes swept the sea.

"How will we know where we are without a map?" Lilly asked in an even smaller voice.

"Where we are? That's easy, dearie," said Mrs. Teagarden. "We're lost."

Lost at Sea

Lilly forgot about finding a rock on which to be put ashore. "Didn't you say you knew the way to the Shipwreck Islands?"

"Well, dearie, as I recall, I didn't exactly tell ye I did. Thought Aristotle might, but all he says is 'Bring her about' and 'Twenty degrees to port.' Besides which, ye might say we're not exactly lost. We know where *we* are. We jist don't know where the Shipwrecks are. And there's not a better place to be than the open sea."

"But what about Momma and Poppa?"

"Don't ye fret, dearie. We'll find 'em. Soon as we find the Shipwrecks."

Why, oh, why had she ever come to sea? Why had

she trusted a pirate? What if even now her momma and poppa had been rescued somehow? What if they were sailing back to Mundelaine and Lilly wasn't there because she was lost at sea?

"I thought you knew what we were doing," she said. "I trusted you."

Mrs. Teagarden squinted at the horizon. "Aye, well, that's a problem, trusting pirates. Even if ye're a pirate yerself. Got to look out for yerself, ye do. But don't ye worry, dearie, I'll get us there. If we sail long enough, we're bound to run into something. If we don't run out of food first."

She fished in the pocket of her apron and pulled out a crumpled bag. "Hardtack," she said. "Good for what ails ye."

Lilly shook her head. Just the thought of eating made her want to toss her cookies. If she had any cookies left to toss, which she didn't.

Mrs. Teagarden crunched her way through what looked like a lumpy rock. Lilly looked away. But what was there to look at? The open sea. The sea upon which they were lost and farther than ever from Momma and Poppa.

From the front of her dress, Mrs. Teagarden pulled out the green glass bottle and took a sip. Then she yawned. "Time for me to catch some shut-eye," she said. "Seeing as how there's no one after us, time for ye to take the tiller and steer. Anyways, it's the only sure cure for seasickness."

Lilly knew what would happen if she took that long stick, that tiller, in her hands and tried to steer the boat. They would die, all of them, even if she wrote the worry down a hundred times in her worry book first. They would drown, and Momma and Poppa would die, because no one except Lilly and Mrs. Teagarden knew they were shipwrecked in the Shipwreck Islands.

Mrs. Teagarden hoisted Lilly up on wobbly legs and thrust the long stick of wood into Lilly's hand. Lilly's wet-noodle fingers refused to wrap around it. "I can't," she quavered.

"Is that any way for a pirate to talk? Ye're no good to anyone hanging over the side and feeding the fish yer dinner. And besides, if ye don't do what the captain says, that's mutiny, that is. And ye know what happens to mutineers, don't ye?"

Lilly shook her head.

"As captain of the ship I kin maroon ye on the nearest bit of land, with naught to eat but yer seabag and yer shoes," said Mrs. Teagarden. "After a while, even yer shoes'll be tasting good to ye." Lilly looked around.

Not a speck of land in sight. Being on solid ground, any solid ground, was what she had yearned for just hours earlier. But not to be left behind, with nothing but the sea for company and her shoes for dinner. Would Mrs. Teagarden even come back for her? Lilly shuddered. She would just have to try to steer the ship. Maybe Mrs. Teagarden wouldn't sleep for long.

Mrs. Teagarden's fingers clenched around Lilly's and pushed the tiller to one side. The boat tilted. Lilly's feet slid toward the edge of the boat. Water gushed in over the side. Mutiny or no, Lilly screamed.

"*Awk! Cluck!* Prepare to abandon ship!" croaked Aristotle from the top of the mast.

Mrs. Teagarden eased back on the tiller, and the boat righted itself again. "See?" she said. "Nothing to it. Push it this way, it goes that way. Push it that way, it goes this way. Even a coconut could sail this boat if it had to. Smarter than a coconut, ain't ye?" She let loose of Lilly's fingers. "Now ye try it."

"But what about the water that came in? We'll sink," Lilly wailed.

"Goes right out that little scupper there, see?" Mrs. Teagarden pointed to an opening in the rail around the edge of the boat. "Ye'd have to try awfully hard to sink the boat that way."

Lilly had no intention of trying. She pushed the tiller the tiniest bit to one side. The front of the boat shifted ever so slightly. No water gushed in. The boat didn't turn over. And her stomach did feel a little less queasy. Like a flying fish, Lilly's heart leaped. Maybe she could do this after all. She hadn't drowned anyone. Yet.

"Where am I heading for?" Lilly asked.

"Well, usually I'd tell ye to steer for a point of land, or a star, if it was a clear night and all, or a cloud. But being as we're lost, and it's not night, and the sky is mostly gray, I'd say jist hold her steady as she goes. That means straight ahead. Don't move the tiller either way."

"What if I turn the boat over?"

"Can't," said Mrs. Teagarden. "Not that sorter boat."

"What if I get us more lost?" Lilly asked.

"Lost is lost." Mrs. Teagarden wrapped herself in her shawl and settled into the bottom of the boat. "I been lost more times than a fish has scales. But I nivver stayed lost. If ye jist keep sailing, ye're bound to end up somewheres." In a moment she was snoring, her snores rising and falling with the waves.

Lilly bit her lip. She held the tiller rigid, moving it not an inch to the left or the right. The wind blew gently on the sail. The boat skimmed over the water. As the moments passed and the boat didn't sink, Lilly felt a

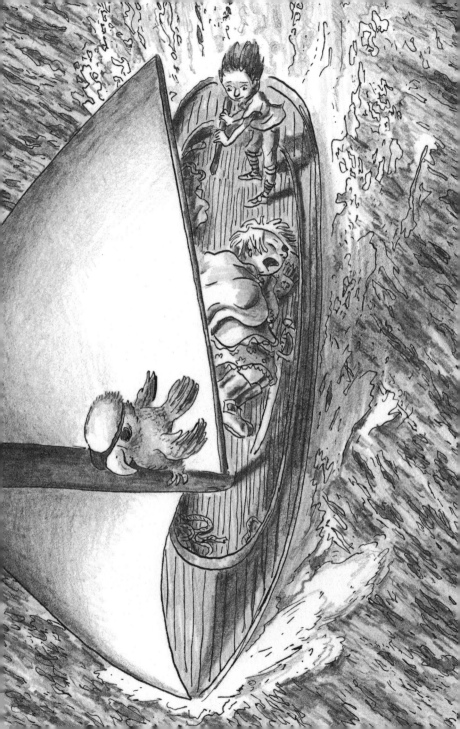

little braver. She could do this. Like Millicent Murray, she could do what needed to be done.

Besides which her stomach seemed to be staying put, not heaving or tossing. Maybe Mrs. Teagarden was right about taking the tiller.

Lilly tore her eyes away from the horizon for a second. Mrs. Teagarden curled in a heap in the bottom of the boat, her shawl around her like a blanket. Who was she, anyway? A pirate—or so she said. Someone who loved sailing, that was clear. Someone Lilly could trust? It was too late to think about that now. Whoever Mrs. Teagarden was, Lilly was stuck with her.

On and on they sailed, Lilly holding the tiller steady, Mrs. Teagarden snoring, Aristotle perched up on the mast with the wind ruffling his feathers.

"*Awk! Cluck!* Steady as she goes!" he squawked every so often.

With every wave that didn't overturn them, Lilly felt a little bit braver, a little bit stronger, a little bit (just the littlest) as though she were flying. Once, she even caught herself humming the tune she had heard Mrs. Teagarden singing in the night. If Millicent Murray could only see her now!

"I'm coming, Momma. I'm coming, Poppa," she whispered, and the wind snatched away her words.

Still, one corner of her mind made lists of new worries to write in her book the first chance she got. She patted her shirt just to make sure the worry book was still safely tucked inside.

When at last Mrs. Teagarden snorted, stirred, and raised herself up on her elbow, Lilly sighed with relief. She had done it. She had sailed the boat. Now she could relax and let Mrs. Teagarden handle everything. Now, at last, she could write and write in her worry book.

"Good work, matey," Mrs. Teagarden said, yawning. "Anything happen whilst I was asleep?"

"Nothing at all," said Lilly, feeling a twinge of pride. "Only that funny little cloud on the horizon behind us. It's been there awhile."

Mrs. Teagarden shielded her eyes and squinted at the horizon. She frowned and rummaged in the front of her dress for a long spyglass.

When she put the spyglass down, her face was grim. "That's not a cloud, dearie," Mrs. Teagarden said. "That's a sail. Someone's chasing us."

Pursued

Mrs. Teagarden pulled on one of the ropes, and the boat leaned far to one side and leaped ahead over the water. Lilly gripped the tiller and shrieked.

"Jist hold her steady," shouted Mrs. Teagarden.

Farther and farther the boat leaned. Spray pounded Lilly. She squeezed her eyes shut. This was it. They would all go down to—where was it?—David Jones's Locker Room. What had even made her think she could sail the boat?

A rough hand covered Lilly's. "Ye done good," said Mrs. Teagarden. "But now we need to make some time."

Lilly opened one eye. Great, smashing waves splashed against the side of the boat. Spray soaked them. But the boat wasn't sinking. Not yet.

Lilly pried her fingers loose and let Mrs. Teagarden take the tiller. "Why are we leaned so far over?" she whispered.

"*Heeled*, dearie, not *leaned*. Ye've got to talk sailor now ye're a pirate. The front of the boat is the bow. The back's the stern. This here is starboard to the right and port to the left. The edges of the boat are the gunwales. And we're heeled over hard to starboard so's we kin go faster and lose that dirty sea dog behind us."

Lilly looked back. Was the sail in the distance closer? "Who do you think it is?" she asked.

"Who else but Blackheart, blast his ears. He'll do anything to get ahold of Aristotle and the treasure of William Barnacle."

"Does Aristotle really know where it is?" asked Lilly.

Mrs. Teagarden shrugged. "Might be he'll lead us to it when we reach the Shipwrecks."

A gust of wind rattled the sails. Mrs. Teagarden pulled on the tiller a bit more, the boat leaned, no, heeled even more. Lilly held her breath. This was it! They were going over. They were doomed.

Then the gust passed, and the boat settled back to its breakneck pace.

On and on they tore. Mrs. Teagarden rummaged in

a corner of the boat and found a bottle of water. She took a swig, then passed the bottle to Lilly. The water washed the sour taste out of Lilly's mouth. This time when Mrs. Teagarden offered her some hardtack, she took it. She wasn't sure she wanted to put any food in her treacherous stomach, but she had to admit she was hungry, when just a while ago she thought she would never be hungry again.

Lilly nibbled at the hardtack. It was hard, all right, hard enough to drive nails with. Behind them, the sail grew larger, no matter how much Mrs. Teagarden fiddled with the ropes or how far over she heeled the boat.

Now if ever was the time for Lilly to write in her worry book. Never had she worried about so many things at once. Luckily this worry book was waterproof. Her parents, who often took field notes in the rain, had given it to her.

Writing with one hand gripping the edge of the boat and the waves knocking the boat around was a challenge. Lilly tried to write small, but the constant up and down of the boat made the letters large and loopy. And no sooner did she start to write a worry down than Mrs. Teagarden ordered her to pull on a line or let a line loose. Finally Lilly put her book away. Her worries would have to wait.

Night fell, hiding their pursuers behind them. Lilly slept fitfully in the bottom of the boat while Mrs. Teagarden steered on and on. Lilly awoke once to Aristotle's squawking and a night ablaze in stars as big as chrysanthemums. Behind the boat, in its wake, the sea twinkled like a line of fire.

Day dawned. The sailboat that followed them loomed large, drawing closer and closer. Its sails were bigger than the ones on the *Last Chance*, and the person steering the other boat looked as though he had tiny sails attached to his head. Lilly recognized the Brusshes salesman. Someone else was in the boat with him, someone with a red bandanna tied around his head, someone who looked familiar.

"Curse his ears," Mrs. Teagarden swore. "That's what makes him such a rum sailor. He kin always tell how to coax more speed out of the wind. On a windy day, the captain used to stand Blackheart in the bow of the boat and order him to take off his hat. We'd pick up half a knot of speed when the wind hit his ears. They let him know which way the wind is blowing, see? He jist trims his sails to his ears, and Bob's yer uncle."

Uncle! Suddenly Lilly remembered Uncle Ernest on the dock, calling her name. She squinted at the other person in Blackheart's boat.

"Can I borrow your spyglass?" she asked Mrs. Teagarden. Steering one-handed, Mrs. Teagarden fished it out of the front of her dress. The boat heaved and bucked on the waves, so Lilly could hardly see through the eye of the lens. The spyglass focused on sail, mast, water, boot buckle. Finally Lilly caught a glimpse of the other sailor. Uncle Ernest stared back at her.

Prepare to Be Boarded!

The boat dipped into a wave. Sea and sky bobbed wildly in the spyglass. Lilly struggled to find the other sailor again. Had she been mistaken? No, there he was, waving his arm at her, an Uncle Ernest Lilly had never seen. In his red bandanna, with a two-day beard, he looked nothing like the Uncle Ernest she knew, except for his gray pajamas.

Had Uncle Ernest been a pirate all along, disguised as a librarian? Uncle Ernest, with his gray house and his *Guide to a Visit from Your Great-Niece* and tofu for supper night after night? Even Millicent Murray could not have come up with a better disguise. If it was a disguise. Was Uncle Ernest after the treasure of William

Barnacle, too?

Or was Uncle Ernest coming to rescue her somehow and take her back to Mundelaine, back to safe and solid land? But then what? Even if he was a librarian disguised as a pirate instead of a pirate disguised as a librarian, would Blackheart let them go? And if Uncle Ernest took her back to Mundelaine, Momma and Poppa might never be rescued. Lilly's thoughts spun.

And what about Blackheart? Lilly couldn't imagine him coming to rescue Lilly. He was after the treasure, wherever it was.

Mrs. Teagarden might be a pirate, but she had promised, pirate to pirate, to help Lilly. Mrs. Teagarden had found them a boat. She hadn't sunk them. Yet. She had said she would take Lilly to the Shipwrecks, assuming, of course, that they got unlost. At least with Mrs. Teagarden, Lilly had a chance of finding her momma and poppa again.

Lilly handed the spyglass back to Mrs. Teagarden, who tucked it down her dress. "Can't we go faster?" Lilly asked.

"I'm sailing for all I'm worth, dearie," said Mrs. Teagarden.

The boat heeled over so far, Lilly clung to the high side to keep from sliding out of the boat feet first. On one side of the *Last Chance*—was it starboard?—Blackheart drew steadily nearer, ears flapping. Uncle Ernest shouted and waved, but the wind tore his words away.

Nearer and nearer the other ship drew. Lilly's heart hammered. She didn't need the spyglass to see what was happening now. Blackheart handed the tiller to Uncle Ernest and grabbed something from the bottom of his boat. A big iron hook on the end of a rope.

"*Awk!* Prepare to be boarded!" squawked Aristotle.

"Grappling hook!" screamed Mrs. Teagarden. "Grab the cutlass!"

Lilly looked wildly around. Mrs. Teagarden's sword belt lay on a heap of sail in the front, no, the bow of the boat. Gingerly she picked up the sword belt and pulled out the sword. "Now what?" she screamed over the wind.

"When he throws the hook, cut the rope!" shouted Mrs. Teagarden. "Or run him through, if ye'd rather. Messy, though. I'd go for the rope if I were ye."

The rope. She would try to cut the rope.

Closer and closer the boat drew. The wind howled. Waves churned. Clouds seethed.

"Squall off to port!" shouted Mrs. Teagarden. "If we keep this course it should miss us." The storm kept pace with them. Across the water they tore, two ships and a squall. Lilly didn't know which to worry about more—death by pirates (even if one was her great-uncle) or death by storm.

Clunk!

The *Last Chance* shuddered and slowed, the iron hook buried in the gunwale. Blackheart pulled on the rope, drawing his boat nearer and nearer.

"Now!" shouted Mrs. Teagarden. "Cut the rope!"

Lilly swung the cutlass. It glanced off the thick, tarry rope.

"Harder!" screamed Mrs. Teagarden.

"*Awk! Awk!* Put yer back into it!"

Lilly swung again. The sword cut into the rope. A few strands parted.

And Blackheart was almost alongside them now, hauling on the rope.

Desperately, Lilly sawed with the cutlass. Just as Blackheart's hairy hand reached to grab the side of their boat, the last strands of rope parted. Blackheart clamped his hand hard on their boat and kept pulling closer.

Lilly couldn't stab him. She couldn't.

But she could turn the cutlass so the handle pointed down, and she smacked his knuckles hard.

"Yeow!"

Suddenly the *Last Chance* leaped forward again.

Lilly tumbled down into the bottom of the boat. By the time she sat back up, the other boat was falling behind, Blackheart sucking on the knuckles of one hand and waving his other fist in the air. The ugly iron hook still lay buried in the side of their boat.

"Shake out yer sails!" squawked Aristotle above the howling wind.

"They'll catch us again soon," said Mrs. Teagarden. "We'll nivver outrun them, but there's one place Blackheart's ears won't help him. Duck, dearie, so the boom don't hit ye."

Lilly ducked.

Mrs. Teagarden unwrapped a rope wound around a piece of metal on the edge of the boat. "Ready about, hard alee!" she cried and pushed the tiller hard to one side. The boat stopped dead in the water, sails flapping. Blackheart's boat surged up so close beside them, Lilly could have reached out and grabbed Uncle Ernest's hand. Then the wind caught their sails, the *Last Chance* skewed around, and Lilly and Mrs. Teagarden tore off in a different direction.

Straight into the storm.

So That's Why They Call It a Boom!

Before Lilly had time even to think a worry, black clouds boiled around them. Lightning splintered the waves, which rose up black and foaming, higher than the bow of the boat. Rain hammered. Lilly was instantly soaked to the skin. The wind drove the boat so far over on its side that water poured in.

"*Awk!* Batten the hatches!" shrieked Aristotle.

"We're sinking!" screamed Lilly.

Mrs. Teagarden did something with the tiller, and the boat righted itself. Lilly breathed a sigh of relief.

Then Mrs. Teagarden jammed the tiller into Lilly's hands.

Lilly snatched her hands away. The boat lurched. The sails flapped madly.

"Take the tiller!" Mrs. Teagarden shouted.

"I can't!" screamed Lilly. "I don't know what to do in this much wind! I'll drown us all."

"Jist hold her steady for a minute!" Mrs. Teagarden shouted over the wind. "I've got to take in sail!" She planted Lilly's hands back on the tiller, climbed up on the side of the boat, and, rocking wildly with the waves, did something complicated with ropes until the sail looked smaller than before. Lilly clung to the tiller.

"Too much sail for this wind!" Mrs. Teagarden shouted down over the noise of the storm. "But that's a blessing. Blackheart will never sail into this storm. His ears couldn't take it." Just as she made to jump back into the boat, the wind clocked around behind them and gave the sail a mighty shove. The boom that held the sail out to catch the wind hit Mrs. Teagarden with a mighty *thwack*.

Mrs. Teagarden teetered out over the waves. In toward the boat. Out. In.

If Mrs. Teagarden fell into the sea, Lilly could never

rescue her. And then the boat would overturn in the storm and be dashed on the rocks and they would all die and it would all be Lilly's fault and she would never again see her dear momma and poppa. Or ever figure out what she wanted to be. She would be fish food, that was all.

Out. In. Out. In.

Lilly leaned hard on the tiller to hold the boat steady.

Out— In—

The wind caught Mrs. Teagarden's skirt and snagged it on the iron hook.

When she teetered out again, the hook hauled her back. With a *whomp* she tumbled in a heap into the bottom of the boat. Had she hit her head? Was she dead? Mrs. Teagarden dead was as much of a disaster as Mrs. Teagarden lost at sea. A sob shook Lilly. Her hands froze to the tiller. She couldn't let go. They would overturn. And drown. What should she do?

"*Awk!* Steady as she goes!" squawked Aristotle.

Groaning, Mrs. Teagarden sat up in the bottom of the boat. Lilly could have hugged her, she was so glad to see her alive, but she kept her hands glued to the tiller. Any minute now Mrs. Teagarden would take the tiller back. Time enough for Lilly to hug her then.

Mrs. Teagarden shifted her shoulder and grimaced. Even through the sheets of rain, her face looked gray with pain. "Me shoulder's hurt. Don't think we'll have to amputate, though."

Lilly felt faint. Even Millicent Murray had never had to perform an amputation.

Mrs. Teagarden unwrapped her soaking shawl from her shoulders and worked it into a sling. "Ye'll have to sail us through this storm, dearie," she said. "It's that or drown. I'll tell ye what to do. For now, jist hold her steady as she goes."

Lilly hunched over the tiller. Even in her wildest worries, she had never imagined having to steer a boat through a storm at sea. When this nightmare was over— if it was ever over, if she ever found her momma and poppa—she would write everything down in her worry book so that it never, ever, ever could happen again. If only she'd been writing all along, while they sailed. But how would she even have known what to write? Now she knew: *What if I get lost at sea? What if Mrs. Teagarden gets hurt? What if a pirate attacks us? What if a storm tosses us around?* But she hadn't imagined those things before they happened, so how would she ever guess what to worry about next?

Lilly gripped the tiller and peered into the driving rain, the shrieking wind, the waves high as mountains. Tears streamed down her face.

"Steady as she goes," she whispered. "Steady as she goes."

The Teeth of the Storm

The *Last Chance* struggled on. Wind tore at the sails, then gusted even harder. Mrs. Teagarden shouted instructions. With an old bucket she bailed one-handed, trying to help the scuppers keep up with the torrents of rain and seawater pouring in. A bedraggled Aristotle clung to her shoulder.

Lilly's legs ached. Her arms ached. Cold rain beat on her face and filled her eyes. She tasted salt. Was it sea spray or tears? It didn't matter. They were doomed by the storm and the waves and the vastness of the sea, no matter how many times Lilly imagined writing her worries down. Some worries were too big to guard against, no matter what she did.

The storm went on forever. Lilly couldn't remember a time she hadn't been gripping the tiller, rocking with the boat, struggling to hold the tiller steady.

The wind gusted even harder. "Head 'er up!" Mrs. Teagarden yelled. "That means push harder so she goes into the wind."

Lilly gritted her teeth and pushed harder on the tiller. The boat heeled even more.

When the gusts let up, Mrs. Teagarden shouted, "Fall off! Fall off!"

Lilly stared at her with horror. Had Mrs. Teagarden gone crazy? Even if it was mutiny, Lilly wasn't going to fall off the boat on purpose, no matter what Mrs. Teagarden said.

"That means ease up a bit on the tiller," Mrs. Teagarden hastily explained.

Lilly eased up on the tiller.

Head up. Fall off. Head up. Fall off. So many waves washed over them that it seemed they were sailing under the ocean instead of on top of it. On and on they sailed, drenched to the bone. Was it night or day? Lilly couldn't tell in the darkness of the storm. She had been sailing in this boat all her life, would sail in this boat all the rest of her life.

At least Mrs. Teagarden knew what to tell Lilly to do. Mrs. Teagarden might even be as good a sailor as Millicent Murray was in *Millicent Murray and the Sea Gull That Didn't Screech*. After a while, some sense of what she was doing seeped into Lilly's numb brain. Her legs braced with the gusts. She leaned into the tiller when the bow of the boat dived down a gigantic wave, let the tiller push back as they climbed up the green foaming mountains.

Her heart still rose in her throat when the boat heeled, but the boat really did right itself. Lilly didn't have to think so hard about what to do. She didn't have to think about what Millicent Murray would do. It was as though some secret part of Lilly, so secret even she didn't know about it, harbored a sailor who knew how to handle a boat. Head up. Fall off. Head up. Fall off. Steady as she goes. Maybe, like finding her sea legs, she was finding a sea heart as well.

And then it was over.

They sailed out of the edge of the storm. The rain stopped. The wind eased to a steady push. Behind them the clouds roiled on. Waves still rose around them like sea mountains, but sunlight sparkled on their tops, and the little boat rode them bravely up one side and then swooped down the other. Lilly shoved her wet hair out of her eyes and looked around. She had sailed through the storm! And she hadn't killed them at all. Millicent Murray could not have done better.

Where were they? Lilly had no idea. And for once she didn't even think to worry about it. They were alive. That was enough. A little laugh escaped Lilly's lips.

Mrs. Teagarden grinned at her. "Aye, we'll make a sailor out of ye yet," she said.

One by one, Lilly pried her fingers loose and shook out first one hand, then the other. Aristotle shook out his wet feathers and flew up to the mast. Lilly looked around. No sign of Blackheart or Uncle Ernest anywhere. She hoped the storm hadn't sunk them.

"Land ho! Dead ahead. *Awk!*" Aristotle squawked.

Mrs. Teagarden struggled to her feet.

The boat rose up on another wave. From its peak Lilly saw a line of islands, shimmering in the sun, surrounded by turquoise sea. Green palm trees swayed in the wind. Waves washed sandy beaches. The sweet scent of flowers blew past her nose.

"Is it the Shipwrecks?" she asked as the boat rushed down the other side of the wave. Were they really so close to finding Momma and Poppa?

"Aye, that it is," said Mrs. Teagarden. "Ye sailed us right to them."

"But they're beautiful," Lilly cried. "I thought they would be terrible."

"Aye, that's their treachery," said Mrs. Teagarden. "Ye're lured in by the outer islands, all green and gorgeouslike. But right behind the shore, it's desert and rock, all barelike. And the reason they call them the Shipwrecks—"

Crash!

"—is because of all the rocks around them ye can't see," Mrs. Teagarden shouted as the boat broke apart and water rushed in and closed over Lilly's head.

Into the Drink

Water everywhere. Water in her nose, her ears. Water pushing her down. Water swallowing her. This was it! The end of everything. Almost her worst worry in the world.

Lilly squeezed her eyes shut. If she was going to drown, at least she wouldn't have to watch. She felt a wave lift her up, up, up. Her head broke the surface of the water. For an instant she opened her eyes. Water, water, nothing but water. Lilly spat out salty water and gulped air before another wave tumbled her under again.

Which way was up? Up to sweet, sweet air?

If only she had listened when her momma and poppa had tried to teach her to swim. Lilly had made up her own rule about swimming: stay far, far away from the water. But that rule wasn't going to help her now, here, in the middle of the ocean.

Up, gasp for air. Down, squeeze eyes shut. The waves tossed Lilly. Her arms flailed. Her legs kicked wildly. From the top of a wave she caught a glimpse of an island in the distance. Was it one of the Shipwrecks? But it was far too far away to do Lilly any good.

The sea had taken Lilly's parents, and now it had come for her. *Farewell, Momma*, Lilly thought as the water closed over her head again. *Farewell, Poppa*. And as an afterthought, *Farewell, Mrs. Teagarden. Farewell, Uncle Ernest.*

Farewell, sweet world, she added. Millicent Murray had said something like that once when she thought all was lost.

Millicent Murray! What would she do?

Get rid of anything holding her down. That's what she'd done in *Millicent Murray and the Hurricane That Didn't Howl*. That's how Millicent Murray had stayed afloat until the Cuban shrimp boat had rescued her, and she had fixed shrimp flambé and tuned their boat engine to run on coconut oil.

Lilly kicked off her shoes.

Still sinking. But a little slower.

The books!

Lilly fumbled in her shirt. *Millicent Murray and the Hyena That Didn't Laugh*. The pages were too wet to read, and Lilly practically knew it by heart anyway. She dropped the book into the watery depths. *Millicent Murray and the Rooster That Didn't Crow* checked out from the Mundelaine library. Lilly hesitated, then let the book fall. If she ever saw Uncle Ernest again, she would just have to make things right with him somehow.

Lilly was rising slowly.

Too slowly.

All that still weighed her down was her worry book. Lilly clutched it. How could she let it go to a watery grave? Maybe she and her worry book could stay afloat together. Lilly's head broke the surface.

Another wave crashed over Lilly. Down, down, down she went. She had only one choice.

Lilly opened her fingers.

The worry book floated out of her hand and began its journey to the bottom of the sea. Lilly imagined it sinking slowly, slowly through the green depths. Maybe fish would nibble its pages as it rested on the ocean floor.

Lilly was rising, rising . . .

Her head broke the surface. She gasped in a lungful of sweet, sweet air.

She was alive!

The waves carried Lilly down, up, down, up, but now, like a floating cork, her head stayed above water. What was it Mrs. Teagarden had said to do if the ship sunk? Grab on to something. But what? Everything was water.

Down, up.

Down, up.

Did she have enough strength to keep on bobbing until the waves washed her to land? At the top of each wave she looked for the islands, but they never seemed any closer. Maybe the waves would win in the end and carry her down where her worry book had gone. At least for now, she wasn't drowning. At least her head was above water.

Something landed on Lilly's head. She went under.

Lilly kicked wildly. The weight lifted off her head, and she surfaced.

"*Awk!* SOS! SOS!"

Aristotle!

Aristotle hovered in front of Lilly's nose. He flapped off, then flew back again. "Mayday! Mayday! *Awk!*" Aristotle squawked.

The next wave lifted Lilly high in the air. From its

top she could see where Aristotle was trying to lead her. Not toward the island at all.

Two waves over, Mrs. Teagarden floated, her skirt open around her like an enormous flower. It had trapped enough air to keep her afloat. Her injured arm, knotted in the sling of her shawl, was useless for swimming.

Lilly lost sight of Mrs. Teagarden as the wave she was riding dove down, then carried her up again. Mrs. Teagarden was definitely riding lower in the water. The air must be leaking out of her skirt.

Lilly might not be drowning, but Mrs. Teagarden was.

Things That Go Bump in the Ocean

Lilly flailed her arms and kicked her legs in the direction she had last seen Mrs. Teagarden. The wave sank down, then rose up again. Was she any closer? Lilly couldn't tell. Aristotle flapped above her, showing the way. Lilly kicked harder. She reached out and grabbed water, pulled it toward her. She was swimming, sort of.

Up, flail, grab, kick. Down, flail, grab, kick. She was getting the hang of it now. Up, flail, grab, kick. Down, flail, grab, kick.

Bump.

Something knocked against Lilly's foot. She screamed and pulled her legs up into a ball.

Bump, bump. Something dark was rising to the surface. Something much bigger than Lilly. Maybe, if she held very still, whatever it was would think she was just a piece of driftwood or a bunch of seaweed and ignore her.

Bump.

Lilly gave up on holding still and swam harder. Her arms and legs worked amazingly well when she was scared.

The something nudged Lilly. She squeezed her eyes shut and waited to be eaten.

Bump, bump.

No teeth. No claws. She wasn't being eaten. Not yet, anyway. Lilly opened one eye a crack. A piece of a boat floated next to her. There were letters painted on it: st Ch. No sea monsters. No carnivorous seaweed. Only a lovely, lovely piece of the boat, come to save her. As long as she could hold on to the wood, she was safe. It tipped a bit as Lilly grabbed hold, but it floated on top of the waves.

"Bring her about. *Awk!*"

Lilly kicked harder, steering the piece of wood after

Aristotle. At the top of the next wave, she could see Mrs. Teagarden down below. Up and down. Up and down. Each time Lilly could see Mrs. Teagarden from the top of the wave, her bubble of skirt had sunk lower into the ocean.

"Hang on!" Lilly cried. "I'm coming." She kicked harder still. A wave picked her up and raced her down its side just as Mrs. Teagarden sank again beneath the surface. Lilly let go of the wood with one hand and grabbed for Mrs. Teagarden. Her fingers clutched hair. Lilly tugged. The hair came up in her hands like a small, wet animal.

Lilly shrieked.

Then she realized she was holding a wig. Of course. Part of Mrs. Teagarden's disguise.

Lilly tossed the wig away. Clutching her raft of wood with one hand, she felt around with the other. Nothing.

No time to think. No time to worry. Only one thing to do.

Lilly took a deep breath, squinched her eyes shut, let go of the wood, and sank beneath the water. She flapped her arms, feeling for Mrs. Teagarden. Nothing.

Lilly bobbled up for air. The wood still bobbed next to her.

Down she went again. This was no time to think about the dangers she might see underwater—giant sharks, rabid barracudas, drowned sailors in David Jones's Locker Room. Lilly opened her eyes to look for Mrs. Teagarden.

Sun shimmered down through the water, all lines and ripples of green. It was so beautiful Lilly almost gasped. But she remembered to keep her mouth shut, remembered to look for Mrs. Teagarden. Something pink wavered at the edge of her sight. A giant jellyfish? Lilly's heart stuttered, but she kept looking. No, it was the fringe on Mrs. Teagarden's shawl.

Lilly grabbed for the fringe and kicked hard. The weight of Mrs. Teagarden pulled Lilly down.

She kicked harder.

And harder.

Slowly, slowly, Mrs. Teagarden started to rise toward the surface.

Lilly's lungs were bursting. Should she let go and save herself?

Never! With one mighty kick, Lilly broke through the surface and sucked in air, looked for the raft.

There! Lilly grabbed the wood with one hand and hauled hard with the other. Like a whale surfacing, Mrs.

Teagarden broke through the waves. Lilly tugged her toward the raft. The waves washed them closer. Lilly felt as if she were towing a ship through the sea. She tightened her grip.

Aristotle flapped above her. "Man overboard!" he shrieked. "Dead man's float!"

"Please," Lilly choked. "Please don't be dead."

Land Ho

The makeshift raft tilted and threatened to swamp as Lilly struggled to push Mrs. Teagarden onto it. Finally she crawled onto the raft herself and tugged Mrs. Teagarden on board by her shawl. A wave lifted her up and deposited her on the raft. The wood settled low in the water but stayed afloat.

Mrs. Teagarden lay facedown. Heaving her over might tip the whole raft, and then they would be back in the drink. Lilly didn't have the strength left to rescue them both again.

"Out goes the bad air! *Awk!*" Aristotle flapped in her face.

Of course! Just what Millicent Murray had done in *The Duck That Wouldn't Quack*. She had pushed on the waterlogged rum smuggler's back to start him breathing again.

"In goes the good! *Cluck!*"

Lilly shooed Aristotle away and started to push.

Out goes the bad air.

In goes the good.

What if Mrs. Teagarden drowned?

Lilly pushed the thought away.

Out goes the bad air.

In goes the good.

What if Mrs. Teagarden was all right but they were lost at sea again with only salt water to drink and died of thirst?

Lilly pushed that thought away, too.

Out goes the bad air.

In goes the good.

What if it rained and they had water to drink but they starved to death? What if they had to eat each other a toe at a time to stay alive?

With every push, Lilly shoved another worry away.

Out goes the bad air.

In goes the—

"*A-hack, a-hack, blurble, aargh.*"

"You're alive! You're alive!" Lilly pounded Mrs. Teagarden's back.

"*A-hack, a-hack, a-hooey.* I feel like a drowned sea rat." Mrs. Teagarden dragged herself up. Lilly flung her arms around the pirate. The raft tilted alarmingly.

"Easy now, *a-hack, a-hooey*," warned Mrs. Teagarden, but she gave Lilly a rough one-armed hug back. "Our boat appears to have shrunk some. What happened?"

Lilly scooted away to balance the raft. She could have danced on the waves, she was so happy to see Mrs. Teagarden breathing. "We hit something," Lilly said. "And then we were in the water and I thought I was going to drown, but I dropped my books and I didn't drown, but you looked like you were sinking."

"Right ye were," coughed Mrs. Teagarden.

"And a piece of ship floated up and I got you on and Aristotle told me how to give you artificial respiration and here we are."

"And Bob's yer uncle, eh? Well, thankee, dearie. I would've been done for, I'm afeard, with me arm in this sling. Speaking of which . . ." With one hand, Mrs. Teagarden managed to pull off the shawl, cradling her hurt arm next to her chest. "I don't suppose we have an extra piece of wood around here, do we? No, well, here ye go, dearie." Mrs. Teagarden held out one end of the shawl. "Jist stand up and hold this corner, will ye?"

Lilly barely thought about tipping the raft. If it did tip, if she went into the drink, she would just climb back on again. That's what she would do. And stand up and try again.

Lilly climbed to her feet and held one corner of the shawl. The raft rocked, but Lilly rocked with it. Sea legs, that's what she had. Sea legs and sea arms. And a sea heart. She could feel it beating in her chest.

Mrs. Teagarden held a corner of the shawl with her good arm. She trapped the third corner between her boots, and the shawl billowed and caught the wind. Soon they were skimming up and down the waves. In the distance ahead, Lilly could see green palm trees and white sand.

And in the other direction, still in the distance but definitely headed their way, Lilly saw the sails of Blackheart's boat.

Ashore at Last

The wind wafted them steadily toward shore. Lilly gripped her corner of the shawl. It was an odd feeling, being part of a boat, but Lilly didn't mind it too much. In fact, she rather liked it. Then a worry struck.

"What about rocks?" she asked.

"We don't stick down into the water anymore. Right smart of ye to lose all that extra boat for us," said Mrs. Teagarden.

Lilly leaned far enough over to see into the water without tipping the raft. Huge, jagged boulders lurked under the surface, but Mrs. Teagarden was right. They were sailing right over them.

The wind nudged the raft onto the white sands of the

island. Lilly dropped her end of the shawl and stepped onto dry land. Her knees wobbled.

"Takes a while to get yer land legs back again," said Mrs. Teagarden, heaving herself up off the raft.

Lilly didn't care. If she fell, she would just kiss the ground, she was so happy. Even in her sodden clothes, she felt lighter somehow. As though all her worries had lifted up into the air and flown away. Now all they had to do was find Momma and Poppa. After all she had been through, that didn't sound so hard.

"Welcome ashore," said a voice behind them.

Lilly whirled. A man stood on the shore. He wore a mishmash of clothes—tattered brown breeches, a shirt that looked woven of bark, and a wide hat of coconut fronds ruffling in the wind.

Aristotle flew to the stranger and pecked him gently on the head. "Home at last! Home at last! *Awk!* Checkmate!"

"Aristotle, my old mate." The stranger smoothed Aristotle's feathers. "I see you lost another boat, Emmaline."

Mrs. Teagarden looked up from retying her shawl as a sling. "Aye, that I did, William. Weren't much of a boat, but it was all I could lay me hands on. Desperate situations, ye know."

A smile creased the stranger's face. "Ah, you've read my books, then?"

"Didn't need to," said Mrs. Teagarden. "Ye said it often enough when we was shipmates."

"You were pirates together?" Lilly asked. The stranger didn't look like a pirate. He looked more like a walking coconut tree. But then, Uncle Ernest hadn't looked like a pirate. Come to think of it, Lilly was pretty sure *she* didn't look like a pirate either.

"Aye, we've sailed many a time on the same ship," said Mrs. Teagarden. "I allus was one of his best students, if I do say so meself."

"Except for a habit of losing your ships," said the stranger.

"Now ye can't hold that against me," said Mrs. Teagarden. "I didn't mean to leave ye here when the ship went down, but the tides carried me off. And I'm here now, ain't I? I come back for ye, didn't I?"

"But who are you?" asked Lilly. A dozen questions crowded her brain. She hardly dared to ask the most important question. What if the answer was no?

"Lilly," said Mrs. Teagarden, "meet William Barnacle."

Lilly took a deep breath. "Have you seen my momma and poppa?" she asked. "They came here to study frangipangi fruit flies and were shipwrecked."

"As is almost everyone who tries to land here," said William Barnacle. "I tried to warn them in my book, *The Prudent Mariner's Guide to the Shipwreck Islands.* But scientists will take great risks for knowledge."

"Are they here?" Lilly demanded. "Are they all right?"

"Your parents are here, and they are fine, although worried about how they will sail back to you without a boat."

Lilly's knees gave way. Mrs. Teagarden grabbed Lilly with her good arm. "See, dearie, I told ye they'd be right as rain."

Yes, yes, yes, they were all right. Shipwreck, storm, pirates, nothing else mattered. Her momma and poppa were fine.

"And splendid company, I must say," added William Barnacle. "They are on a nearby island studying frangipangi fruit flies and the reproductive habits of the frangipangi tree. It's a pleasure to have such scholarly guests."

"Take me to them, please," begged Lilly.

"We must wait a bit for the tides to be right," said William Barnacle. "One can cross from island to island only for short intervals at specific times of day and only if one knows exactly where to step. Otherwise the riptides wash you out to sea."

Lilly's insides were jumping up and down. Wait? How could she wait now that she was so close? What if William Barnacle was really lying and her parents weren't safe at all? But he was a scholar. Why would he lie? But he was a pirate, too. Was he holding her momma and poppa for ransom? Forcing them to dig for treasure? Had he made them walk the plank?

"*The Prudent Mariner's Guide* didn't say anything about crossing from island to island," Lilly said.

"Nor would it," said William Barnacle. "Very little is known about these islands, which is why I chose them for scholarly privacy and why I omitted certain facts from *The Prudent Mariner*. For instance, no one knows that between the rocks and the reefs this bay has a deep natural harbor where a boat, if it knew the way, could tie up to shore."

"Well, someone has figured it out," said Mrs. Teagarden, pointing out to sea.

Lilly and William Barnacle turned to look. While

they had been talking, a sailboat had glided into the harbor and tied up to a rock. Leaping ashore, bearing down on them, was Blackheart the pirate. Behind him came Uncle Ernest.

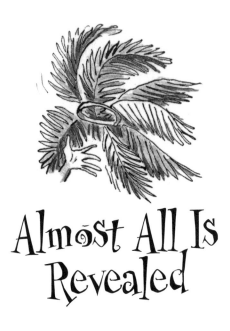

Almost All Is Revealed

I knew that blarsted bird would lead us to William Barnacle and the treasure!" cried Blackheart, sword waving, ears flapping. "Hand over the gold!"

"Lilly, are you all right?" cried Uncle Ernest.

"Prepare to repel boarders! *Awk!*" squawked Aristotle.

"I'm fine, Uncle Ernest," said Lilly. "But what are you doing here?"

"I was awakened by something slamming," said Uncle Ernest. "When I checked on you, you were gone. I looked out the window and saw you being taken away by a disreputable-looking washwoman. I didn't even stop to check *A Guide to a Visit from Your Great-Niece* to see if I should rescue you. When you jumped onto that boat and I saw this gentleman setting off after you, I insisted he take me along to bring you home again."

"Clung to me boat like a squid, he did, until I took him aboard," said Blackheart. "Would have tossed him overboard, except for that book he had with him."

"I had picked up *The Prudent Mariner's Guide to the Shipwreck Islands* when I saw it lying on the dock." Uncle Ernest shook his head. "A shameful way to treat a library book."

Lilly blushed. "I didn't mean to drop it."

"And he could read it, he could," broke in Blackheart. "That's how we found ye after the storm. He read the chart. Almost makes me think there might be some use to book learning. Turned out to be a fair hand with a sail, too."

"Ye nivver were one for reading in pirate school," Mrs. Teagarden said to Blackheart. "Always more interested in yo-ho-hoing."

It was almost too much for Lilly to take in. Uncle Ernest, gray Uncle Ernest, had come to rescue her.

"Have you always been a pirate?" she asked Uncle Ernest.

"Er, no, but I'm afraid I told you an untruth about Mundelaine never having a pirate school. And about no one ever wanting to go to it. I wanted to go more than anything. But my parents sent me off to future librarian's camp, and by the time I came home, the pirate school had been closed by the more narrow-minded townspeople. All these years I thought that perhaps being a librarian was indeed a better choice, but now—"

"Enough of yer jibber-jabber," warned Blackheart. He waved the tattered treasure map. "I know there's treasure here. I wants me treasure!"

William Barnacle stepped forward. "As to the treasure," he began.

"Willie?" asked Uncle Ernest. "Is that you? From Camp Dewey Decimal? I thought you were a palm tree standing there."

William Barnacle pulled off his palm-frond hat and peered at Uncle Ernest. "Ernie? I didn't recognize you. You won Future Librarian of the Week three times in a row."

"I knows who ye both are," roared Blackheart. "And I wants me treasure."

Uncle Ernest and William Barnacle threw their arms around each other's shoulders and broke into song.

> *We are fine librarians*
> *With books upon the shelves,*
> *But never any time to*

Read them for ourselves.
Manuals and mysteries,
Cooking books and histories,
Biology, theology,
Fluvial morphology.
From books of enormous size
To books infinitesimal
We catalog them all with
Dewey Dewey Decimal!

"When I found out that librarians didn't simply read books all day long, I decided I had better be a scholar instead," said William Barnacle.

Uncle Ernest looked wistful. "I fear that, due to my unexplained and abrupt absence from my job, I am no longer chief librarian of Mundelaine."

"The treasure!" Blackheart roared, his ears red. "I wants the treasure, and I wants it now. Or I'll be cutting off ears till I gets it."

Lilly's hands went to her ears. After all she had gone through to find Momma and Poppa, had she really just brought them more danger? Would Blackheart really carry out his threat?

152

A Desperate Act

Lilly narrowed her eyes. She could think of only one way to make sure that her momma and poppa would be safe. That all of them and all of their ears would be safe from Blackheart. A desperate way, to be sure.

Voices argued. Arms waved. Blackheart roared. Aristotle squawked. Lilly slipped away unnoticed.

She fumbled with the knot tying Blackheart's ship to a rock on shore. At last it came undone. Lilly hesitated. What if she ruined their only chance of getting off the islands? But this was a desperate situation.

She gave the boat a good push and jumped on board. Her hands knew what to do without her even thinking. She hauled on the rope as she had watched Mrs.

Teagarden do, and the sail pulled taut. Lilly pushed on the tiller. The boat nosed away from the rocks. Wind bellied the sail and pushed Blackheart's boat out into the harbor.

Lilly filled her lungs and shouted, "AHOY, THE SHORE."

Five heads swiveled in her direction.

"Here, now, what're ye doing with me boat?" shouted Blackheart.

"That's me girl!" Mrs. Teagarden cheered.

"The tides are about to turn," warned William Barnacle. "Mind the rocks."

"Ye can't hear the rocks like I kin," added Blackheart.

"Lilly, listen to reason," called Uncle Ernest.

Lilly felt her own piratical heart rise up. It beat in her chest like waves pounding. She held the boat steady to the wind and shouted, "No, you listen to me!

"This is my ship now, and when Momma and Poppa come I'm taking them away with me, and I'll leave all of you here unless you all swear to take orders from me."

"Nivver!" screamed Blackheart. "Nivver, nivver, nivver."

Aristotle flew to the top of the mast. "*Awk!* Marooned!" he squawked. "Bon voyage!"

Shaking, Lilly leaned on the tiller and brought the

boat about. She wouldn't really sail away and leave Momma and Poppa or Uncle Ernest or, for that matter, Mrs. Teagarden or William Barnacle if they wanted to come. But Blackheart had to believe she would. He had to believe she was a pirate now.

"All hands on deck!" squawked Aristotle. "Prepare to raise anchor."

Lilly headed the boat for the open seas.

"Bring me boat back!" shrieked Blackheart. "I'll swear, I will."

The wind obligingly shifted, turned the boat so that it pointed back toward shore, then spilled out of the sails. Blackheart's boat, no, Lilly's boat stood at a standstill too far from shore to be boarded.

"Swear on your honor as pirates and scholars and . . . and librarians!" Lilly called. "Swear the ship is mine and you'll all do exactly what I say."

"I swear as a pirate and a scholar that I will follow your directions," said William Barnacle.

"The *Guide* didn't mention what to do about this," said Uncle Ernest. "But I will swear on my honor as a librarian. And an honorary pirate."

Was that a gleam in his eye? Lilly was too far from shore to be sure.

"And I swears on me honor as a pirate," said Mrs. Teagarden.

Waves gently rocked the boat. Lilly held her breath. What if Blackheart wouldn't swear after all? Then what?

"And mine," Blackheart growled at last. "Me honor as a pirate. But I still wants me treasure."

"And put down your sword so you won't cut off anyone's ears," Lilly ordered.

Blackheart grumbled, but he took off his sword and handed it over, along with his pistols, to William Barnacle.

"Throw him in the brig! *Awk!*" squawked Aristotle.

Lilly let her breath out. Her desperate plan had worked! She turned the boat, her boat, and eased it back to shore. Eight hands grabbed the line she tossed to pull in the boat. Before the boat had been safely tied off, Lilly saw what she most wanted to see. Coming across the sand were the two people Lilly loved best in the whole world. Her momma and her poppa.

Black water still lapped between boat and rocks. Lilly didn't care. She leaped.

Reunited at Last

Lilly's feet barely touched the ground before she was running, and her momma and poppa, with gasps of disbelief and joy, were running, too. The wind gave Lilly wings, lifted her up, flew her straight into their arms. Oh, the hugs! The laughter! The joy! The wind swirled around them in a giddy little whirl.

"Lilly! Lilly!"

"Momma! Poppa!"

"Oh, Lilly, we've been so worried about you. Did you get our note that we were all right?"

"I must have left before it came," said Lilly, hugging them even tighter. "All the homing sea gulls came at once and Mrs. Teagarden said you must be shipwrecked and we should come save you and we got lost and I sailed us through a storm and we were shipwrecked."

"And we were worried sick about how we would get back to you," said her poppa.

"And I made everyone promise that Blackheart's boat is mine so we can sail back to Mundelaine." Lilly caught her breath.

"And we were so worried about how we would find a boat and come to Mundelaine to bring you here," said Lilly's momma, still hugging Lilly hard.

"Bring me here? But I came to rescue you."

"Oh, Lilly," said her poppa from his side of the hug, "you wouldn't believe these islands. There's so much to study. Not just frangipangi fruit flies. There's frangipangi fruit, and frangipangi fruit bats."

"Years and years and years of study," said Lilly's momma. "It's a scientific paradise. So we thought we could all live together here. At least until you go off to the Scientific Institute."

"About the institute," Lilly began.

"Ahem," said William Barnacle. "I would be remiss in my hospitality if I did not offer you some refreshments. Would you care to step into my abode?"

"Delighted," said Mrs. Teagarden. "Mebbe ye have a drop of rumfustian? I seems to have dropped mine somewheres."

"Most grateful," said Uncle Ernest. "I've had nothing to eat but sea biscuits for several days. You wouldn't have a supply of Dr. Peeler's Health Juice on hand, would you?"

"Uncle Ernest?" For the first time, Lilly's momma looked at someone besides Lilly. "Is that really you?"

"Yes, I fear it is." Uncle Ernest actually smiled at Lilly's momma. "How wonderful to see you, Caroline."

"And you, Uncle Ernest. But what are you doing here? You never travel."

"Well," began Uncle Ernest, shaking the hand Lilly's poppa held out, "when Lilly ran away—"

"Avast and belay the chin-chatter!" shouted Blackheart. "I may not have me boat, but I still wants yer treasure!"

"The treasure is at my hut as well," said William Barnacle.

"Then I'm coming, too," snarled Blackheart.

Lilly held tight to her momma's and poppa's hands and followed William Barnacle through the trees. She had come to rescue her parents, to take them off the islands. What would it be like to live here instead? Balmy weather. Green trees. White sand. The breeze ruffling the palm fronds. And she was with the two people who mattered most in the whole world. Once that would have been all her heart desired. Lilly looked back to where her ship rode the waves. And beyond the ship to the open sea. What did her heart want now?

The Treasure of William Barnacle

William Barnacle's house was a cozy little building of driftwood with coconut fronds for a roof. Inside, on driftwood shelves lining every wall, ceiling to floor, were books and books and books.

"My treasure," said William Barnacle.

"Bilge water!" screamed Blackheart. "Where's the gold?"

"I used it years ago to pay off my library fines," said William Barnacle. Uncle Ernest nodded approvingly.

"*Aaargh!*" snarled Blackheart. "Ye said there was treasure here."

"There is." William Barnacle gestured to the books.

"Double *aargh!*" screamed Blackheart. His ears turned bright red. "I've been hornswoggled."

"What if he decides to steal the boat back?" Lilly whispered to Mrs. Teagarden.

"He won't," Mrs. Teagarden whispered back. "He swore on his pirate honor. Not even a pirate breaks an oath like that."

Reassured, Lilly turned back to the books. One shelf had the familiar red-and-gold spines of Millicent Murray, all thirty-seven of them. And there, right at the end, right after *Millicent Murray and the Fish That Didn't Splash*, was a new volume, *Millicent Murray and the Whale That Didn't Spout*. Lilly wanted to grab the book off the shelf and start reading. Should she steal it? She *was* a pirate now. But she was also Lilly, good as gold for her momma and poppa. Maybe William Barnacle would lend her the book.

"How did you get all of the Millicent Murray books?" Lilly asked. "Where did you find them?"

"Well, the truth is, I don't find them," said William Barnacle. "I write them."

"You? You're the author? Cynthia Sleuthson?"

William Barnacle smiled modestly. "That's my *nom de plume*," he said. "My pen name. Rather clever, don't you think?"

"But I love Millicent Murray. These are the best books in the whole wide world."

William Barnacle blushed bright red. "Not the best, surely. Nowhere near as good as books by Aristophanes or Dickens or, oh, any number of authors I could name. But being a scholar doesn't pay all that well, so I started writing to support my scholarly habits. Even pirates can have dry spells, no ships in sight, nothing to do. One page a day, sent off to my editor by homing sea gull. When a book is published, a flock of sea gulls carries a copy back to me."

William Barnacle sighed. "But now, seeing Emmaline and Blackheart, I've a yen for some pirating again. A little yo-ho-hoing with a trusty crew. But to leave my books . . . It's not easy having a pirate heart and a scholar heart all in the same chest."

Lilly knew what he meant. It wasn't easy either, being a worrier and a pirate. Maybe it wasn't easy for Uncle Ernest to be a librarian and a pirate.

And suddenly the answer to Lilly's question of what her heart wanted flew into her mind as sure as a homing sea gull.

Almost the End

"What if," Lilly asked William Barnacle, "you didn't have to leave your books behind when you went pirating?"

"You mean take them along?" asked William Barnacle. "They would sink the ship with their weight."

"Not if you took only some of them," said Lilly. "Not if you took them around and loaned them to people while you were pirating and then came and got more, and went and got back the ones you loaned and loaned out more."

"A library ship!" cried William Barnacle.

"*Awk!* Your book is overdue," squawked Aristotle.

"But who would be the crew?" William Barnacle asked.

"I would," said Uncle Ernest. "I have taken a liking to the nautical life. Someone would have to see that the library books are cataloged and in alphabetical order and well taken care of—no dog-eared pages, no cracking of the spines. No eating while reading." The ends of his red bandanna quivered. He smiled piratically.

"You're in, mate," cried William Barnacle. He turned to Blackheart. "What about you?"

"Would there be treasure?" he asked.

"There might be," said William Barnacle. "You never know what might happen on the open sea. And at least there'll be fines for overdue books."

"Aye, mebbe I could help ye make sure the dirty dogs pays their fines. And no rotten rapscallion steals any of the words out of yer books."

"Pay or die! Pay or die! *Awk!*"

"And as long as there might be a bit of other pirating as well," added Blackheart.

William Barnacle clapped Blackheart on the back. "Maybe we'll even teach you to read this time around. Emmaline? Will you sign on?"

168

"Aye, well, there's nothing I like better than a deck beneath me feet," she said. "And since me last ship is in Davy Jones's Locker, I reckon I could sail with ye."

"We would need to come back to the Shipwrecks regularly to get more books for the library ship," added Uncle Ernest. "And to visit."

"We would, of course, require a boat," added William Barnacle.

A boat. All heads turned to Lilly. Thanks to her own piratical heart, she owned the only boat on the island.

Lilly's momma and poppa were deep in a discussion of the frangipangi fruit-fly flea. She had just found them. How could she think of leaving them again? Who would keep them safe?

But to sail again on her very own ship with Mrs. Teagarden and Uncle Ernest and William Barnacle, and even Blackheart, with a hold full of books. Lilly's heart rose fiercely. "You can use my boat," she said, "if you take me with you."

"Lilly, are you sure that's what you want?" asked her poppa.

"We would miss you so much," said her momma.

Was she sure? What about all the things that might go wrong while she was gone?

What if . . .

What if Lilly went sailing on her very own boat?

What if her momma and poppa were fine on the island while she was gone?

What if, no matter what happened, everyone would be all right?

"And I'll miss you," Lilly said. "But if I come back to visit twice a month, that's more than you'd see me if I went to the Scientific Institute." She drew a deep breath. "Which I'm not going to," she added.

"Not go to the institute?" asked her momma, perplexed. "But if you're not a scientist, then what will you be, sweetie?"

"I don't know yet," said Lilly. "But I'll find out. Right now I want to go sailing."

"Ye'll come, then?" asked Mrs. Teagarden. "Ye're a right dab hand with the tiller when ye're not tossing yer cookies."

Aristotle settled on Lilly's shoulder. "Prepare to raise anchor! *Awk!* Aye, aye, Captain."

"Are you sure?" asked her poppa again.

Lilly leaned back in the circle of her momma's and poppa's arms. They smiled fondly down on her. To be with them here sometimes. To go sailing whenever she wanted to. What more could Lilly want? And whatever happened, she would find a way to deal with it.

Like Mrs. Teagarden.

Like Millicent Murray.

Like Lilly the pirate.

Lilly herself.

"Yes," Lilly said. "I'm sure."